A GIRL AND HER PANDA

A GIRL AND HER PANDA

ZOEY GONG

Red Empress Publishing
www.RedEmpressPublishing.com

Cover by Cherith Vaughan
www.CoversbyCherith.com

For my sister

CHAPTER ONE

"You're it!" one of the kids yelled as she caught sight of Lihua.

Lihua squealed with laughter as she stood up from her hiding place and looked for the other children. She easily found two other girls who couldn't stop laughing. They jumped up and playfully fought over who would actually be it. The girl who had found Lihua joined the fray, and soon the four of them were fighting and laughing at the same time.

"I think everyone is it!" Lihua said. There was a momentary pause before all of the children burst into screams and they all ran in different directions through the forest looking for whoever had not yet been found.

After a moment, Lihua stopped to catch her breath and found herself completely alone. She turned around and took in the sight of the tall bamboo trees that creaked as they slowly swayed in the breeze. The bamboo forest was so thick, it was nearly dark here, even though it was only mid-afternoon.

She heard a rustling to her left. She took a cautious step toward it.

"Hello?" she called. "Who's there? I won't hurt you." She hoped it was a panda. She had spent her whole life at the edge of a bamboo forest, west of the Dayong Mountains in eastern Bashu. Her grandmother had told her many stories about the fat, fluffy bears that roamed all over the mountains in her girlhood, but Lihua had never seen one.

"The black-footed ghost of the forest," her grandmother called them. They were said to roam the woods, eating anything they could find, even iron pots or bamboo chopsticks. If anything went missing, a panda was surely to blame.

But their pelts were said to be a thing of beauty and even good fortune. So, if a panda were seen, people would kill it and use its fur, bones, and bile as medicine. In recent years, warlords hunted them in large numbers, selling the hides to rich people in the east of the country or even to foreigners.

"When I was a child," her grandmother said. "I would sit in my room on the second floor of our house and watch from my window as the pandas would sneak out of the forest and peek into the village. They would steal our clothes or food. Whatever they could get their wicked paws on."

But Lihua wasn't afraid. At twelve years old, not much scared her.

"Come out," she said as she crept closer to whatever was rutting about in the brush.

She gasped and then sighed in disappointment as a monkey leaped from the ground, scurried up a tree, and joined its many dozens of friends above her. She should have known. It was never a panda.

"Lihua!" Her mother's voice rang through the forest, that shrill, annoyed voice she knew so well.

"Coming!" she called back. She took one last look at the overgrown forest and prayed for just a glimpse of a panda, but her mother's incessant calls did not allow for much hesitation on her part. She finally turned and ran back toward their village.

"Lihua!" her mother scolded as soon as she arrived back home. "Where were you? Lazy girl!"

"It was rest time, but I wasn't tired," Lihua said. "The other children and I—"

"Other children?" her mother interrupted. "All wasteful brats. Each one, so spoiled. Never helping when needed."

"I'm here now, Mama," Lihua said as she pulled on an apron and immediately went to work stoking the fire under the large pot of spicy broth that they used as a base in almost all of the bowls of noodles they served out of their small restaurant.

"Leave the girl alone, Shushu," Lihua's grandmother chastised as she hobbled into the room on her cane. She pulled out a chair and sat down, her face wincing. She then thumbed the bodhi-seed bracelet she always wore as she mumbled to herself.

"How are you feeling, Nainai?" Lihua asked her grandmother.

"Better now that you are here, my pearl," Nainai cooed, but Lihua could always see the pain etched permanently behind her grandmother's eyes.

When Nainai had been a young girl, her feet had been bound, as was tradition for most families. Broken, molded into the desired lotus shape, and then healed in their disfigured form, the girls were unable to walk on their own for very long. But after the death of the Manchu empress, many people—especially the warlords—called for an end to some of the old ways. Nainai's feet were then unbound, but the damage had already been done. The arches of her feet were completely flat, and her toes still curled under. She had once told Lihua that unbinding her feet had been a more painful process than binding them in the first place. She still walked with a limp, when she walked at all.

"Lihua," her mother said, still with her typical sharpness, but with less volume than before now that her mother-in-law was present. "Go check the huajiao and bring them in if they are ready."

"Yes, Mama," Lihua said, and she bounded up the stairs to the roof. The family lived in two rooms above the noodle shop, and they used the roof to store or dry the various fruits, meats, and vegetables they used. Today, they were drying the most recent crop of huajiao—flower peppers, the spicy peppercorns that grew native in their area and gave their food its unique flavor.

The huajiao had been spread out on a large white sheet to dry in the sun. Lihua picked up a huajiao and ran it through her fingers. The hull cracked easily, revealing the sharp-flavored seed inside. She popped the huajiao in her mouth and crushed it between her teeth, letting the spice send its tingling, numbing sensation over her tongue and down her throat. Many people, especially people who were not from Bashu, could not handle the flavor of the huajiao, but Lihua loved it. She was considered a "spicy girl," an affectionate term for girls from Bashu who had built up an immunity to the flavor that could send even the strongest man to his knees, begging for water.

Lihua took a bamboo log and ran it over the dried huajiao. Then she picked up the sheet and poured the huajiao into a finely-woven basket. She stepped to the edge of the roof and shook the basket, letting the chaff separate from the peppercorns and drift away on the breeze. She then put the peppercorns into a jar and went back downstairs.

Without needing to be told, she added more water to the pot of broth, along with garlic, ginger, salt, and some of the freshly-cracked peppercorns. She sipped the broth and added a bit more salt until the flavor was just right. It wasn't quite spicy enough for her taste. If she had her way, she would have added another fistful of peppercorns, but she had learned from experience that if she made it too spicy, the family ended up with unhappy customers. And unhappy customers don't pay. And customers who don't pay created an unhappy Mama. And the last thing Lihua wanted was to make her mother unhappy.

But Mama was always unhappy, it seemed to Lihua. She was older, much older than the mothers of all her friends. She was thin and pale. But she worked hard. She was always working. She was up before dawn and usually the last to lay down for the evening. She worried constantly. Worried about money. Worried about the restaurant. Worried about the warlords. Worried about the future.

Lihua did her best to not cause her mother trouble, but she knew there was little she could do since she had been born a daughter. Eventually, she would marry out and never see her family again. She assumed this was why her mother and father treated her with a coldness, more like an employee than a daughter. They didn't want to become too attached. She knew other girls who were also treated harshly by their families for the same reason. Though, she also knew families who loved and doted on their daughters as well. Sometimes she wished she had a family like that, but she was grateful her parents didn't beat her or treat her cruelly. And she had Nainai. Nainai's love was warm and ever-ready, and more than made up for the lack of affection from Mama.

"Lihua," Nainai called once Lihua was done seasoning the broth. "Come."

She waved Lihua over to her, joss sticks in hand. They walked to the front of the shop and got down on their knees. Nainai handed some of the joss sticks to Lihua and then struck a match, lighting the joss sticks on fire with a spark and sputter. The flame quickly went out, but the sticks continued to burn slowly, releasing its fragrant smoke.

Lihua and Nainai then looked up at the kitchen god over the doorway and kowtowed three times. Then they held their joss sticks in their hands as they closed their eyes and prayed.

Lihua did not know what Nainai prayed for, but Lihua prayed for the same thing she always did: a little brother. Even though the family was rather poor, and a new baby would be a burden for Mama, a boy would help alleviate many of Mama's worries. A boy would never leave them, and eventually, he would bring a daughter-in-law to help Mama run the shop when she was too old.

"Praying again, laoma?" a man said to Nainai with a laugh as he entered the shop, referring to her with the familiar term for an older woman.

"Some reverence from a little pig like you would not go amiss," Nainai said as Lihua helped her stand. Nainai's superstitious nature was almost legendary in their village. Nainai knew every ancestral rite ever imagined, and she practiced all of them.

With the arrival of the first evening patron, the signal for the dinner rush had been given. Lihua helped her grandmother climb the stairs to the room they shared where she could sit out of the way while the rest of the family worked. Lihua then returned to the bowl of broth and put on some noodles to cook in another pot.

Her father arrived soon after with a stack of bamboo logs, each one as thick as a man's arm. He spent much time in the forest, felling and splitting the logs to use for the family's other main dish—rice cooked in bamboo tubes. Her father put rice, meat, huajiao, and other spices into the tubes and sealed them with banana leaves. He then put them on a grill outside and let them cook.

For the rest of the evening, like every other evening of Lihua's life, the family served bowls of noodles and bamboo tubes of rice to countless people who stopped into the shop. Some of the patrons lingered long into the night, drinking baijiu and playing dice. It wasn't until the last of the village's lanterns had burned out that the family finally climbed up the stairs to their rooms and collapsed onto their beds.

Lihua lay by the window and looked up at the stars and moon as she drifted off.

"Lihua..." she heard her grandmother's voice croak from her pallet on the other side of the room.

Lihua sighed as she sat up and folded her hands in front of her to say one last prayer.

"Dear Guanyin," she said, invoking the name of the Goddess of Mercy. "Please send my mother a son."

She was too tired to elaborate or use more fanciful language, but she thought that the goddess must be powerful enough to read the sincerity in her heart. She laid back down and was asleep before her head hit the pillow.

CHAPTER TWO

"And then Ling pushed Zhuang, and he fell back into a mud puddle!" Lihua said with a laugh as she pulled dough into long noodle strands and told her mother about the trouble some of her friends got into that afternoon. "He was so mad! But Ling is much faster, so even though he chased her, she got home before he could reach her, and her dad came outside and threatened to kick Zhuang if he ever—"

"Lihua!" her mother interrupted. "Please..." She didn't finish her request.

Lihua turned and grew concerned when she saw her mother rubbing her forehead. But she was even more surprised to see her mother sitting down! Her mother never took a break. She always just pushed through. Sick, tired, worried. Her mother was always on her feet doing something. To see her mother sitting idle, if even for a moment, caused alarm bells to ring in Lihua's head. She went to her mother's side.

"Are you all right, Mama?" Lihua asked.

Her mother pressed her lips but didn't look at her. "No," she said. "I'm going to have a baby."

It took a moment for the words to sink in, but then Lihua nearly jumped out of her skin in excitement. She tugged on her mother's sleeve.

"Oh, Mama!" she said. "I'm so happy! I prayed for this every day! I know the baby will be a boy!"

Her mother looked at her, her eyes watering. Another first! Her mother never cried.

"You...prayed for us to have a child?" she asked in surprise.

"It is the only thing I ever prayed for," Lihua said, her face beaming.

Her mother looked away and put her hand to her mouth, pinching her eyes shut.

"Mama?" Lihua asked. "What is wrong?"

"What is happening?" Nainai asked as she slowly descended the stairs. Lihua ran to her side and helped her down the last few steps.

"Mama is going to have a baby!" Lihua exclaimed. "My prayers have been answered."

Nainai's face fell as she shot a look at her daughter-in-law. "Is this true?" she asked. The woman nodded. Nainai slowly walked over to a stool and sat down. Lihua then heard the quiet, incessant clanking of her grandmother's bodhi-seed bracelet.

Lihua looked from her grandmother to her mother. She did not understand why the family was not happy. She kneeled by her mother's knee.

"Everything will be fine, Mama," she said. "Guanyin will send you a son. I am sure she will not let him go hungry. The goddess will provide!"

Her mother slapped her hand on the table and sighed

in exasperation as she stood up and went back to work wiping the tables down. “More ridiculous superstitions.”

“Does my son know?” Nainai asked.

“Yes,” Mama said. “He is...looking at options.”

“What do you mean, Mama?” Lihua asked.

“Never you mind,” Mama said. “It doesn’t matter. Maybe the baby won’t come at all. Then nothing will change.”

“Oh, Mama!” Lihua said. “Don’t worry. I’m sure the goddess will protect him.”

“Lihua! Please!” her mother cried, her voice shaking, along with her hands.

Lihua was shocked into silence. What was wrong? Why was her mother so...scared? Angry? Sad? Lihua didn’t understand it. Well, she knew her family would worry about money; they always did. But many poor families had lots of children and they survived. Besides, she was already twelve years old. She could marry in only a couple of years. They could scrape by until then, couldn’t they?

“Please,” her mother said after taking a few deep breaths. She went to the back of the room and looked under a shelf. She pulled out a little jar of money and pulled out some small coins. “Please, go to the market. We need one jin of pork for tonight. Make sure you bargain.”

“Of course, Mama,” Lihua said, taking the coins and a cloth to wrap the meat in. She also took some joss sticks from their box and put them in her pocket. “Can I stop at the temple on the way back? I will pray for the health of the new baby.”

Her mother looked at her with wide eyes. She nodded without a word and then quickly looked away.

As she passed her grandmother, the old woman reached out and grabbed her sleeve.

“Say a prayer for yourself as well, my pearl,” she said.

Lihua gave her a smile and then ran out of the shop toward the market. Why would she say a prayer for herself? Every bit of luck she could muster would need to go to Mama and the baby! She knew that many women died in childbirth, so she would say a prayer for Mama too.

The market was down a narrow alley in the middle of the village. The rank smells infiltrated her nose, but she barely grimaced, she was so used to coming here at least once a day. Filthy ducks and chickens honked and squawked from their wicker baskets. Wriggling fish were lifted from buckets and gutted all along the street. The blood from fresh kills snaked down the road, mixing with the water from the tubs of live frogs and eels. Two dogs barked at each other as they fought over the legbone of a pig someone had carelessly dropped. That bone could have made a good soup, Lihua thought. Stalls of fresh vegetables with bright orange carrots, green lettuce, and purple eggplants made her mouth water.

She finally came to a stall with fresh meat where she knew the vendor would give her the best price.

"Hey, laoban!" she called to the man who ran the stall.

"Little pearl," he said with a smile. Everyone knew her grandmother called her pearl, so other people sometimes called her that as well. "Your cheeks look red. You have been in the sun too much."

"The summer is too hot," she said. "I need to go swim in the river like a fish."

"You'll have to be careful," the man replied. "The river can be very dangerous."

"Do you have good meat for sale today?" she asked, eyeing the bright pink slabs of pork on the table in front of her.

"Of course!" he said. "What? You think I serve garbage?"

"If it will bring you money, I think you might try!" she said jokingly. Friendly insults were always part of the bargaining process.

"You think so?" he asked as he shook a finger at her and then pointed to a fatty piece at the end of the table. "Just to show you how good my pigs are, I will sell you this very high-quality piece right here."

It was a nice piece, but she wrinkled her nose anyway. "Are you trying to sell me last week's rotten meat?"

"What?" he asked, feigning insult. "This is from my best pig! I slaughtered him just for you! I even blessed him before I did it because I knew it would please your grandmother."

Lihua did her best to stifle a laugh. "How much for this old rotten piece?" she asked.

"For you, a very good price." He rattled off a number that was fair, but Lihua didn't want to spend all the money her mother had given her on the meat, even though she was supposed to.

"Why are you trying to rip me off?" she asked, her hands on her hips. "Who else is going to buy this ugly thing from you?"

"Come on, Lihua," he said. "Don't make me beg a little girl for money. I have children to feed."

"I'll tell you a secret if you give me a better price," she said, leaning in. He cocked his head toward her. "My mama is finally going to have a baby!"

"Congratulations!" the man said. "Okay, okay. Just for today, to celebrate your good news, I can give you a special discount. But don't try to haggle with me for the rest of the week, okay?"

"It's a deal!" Lihua said, excitedly handing him only three of the four coins her mother had given her in exchange for the slab of meat. The vendor wrapped the meat up in the piece of cloth she had brought and gave it to her.

"Give your mother my best wishes for a healthy son," he said.

"I will," she said. She ran down the rest of the market street, toward the temple at the end.

She flew past the fortune tellers, the incense sellers, the man who carved ancestor stones, and the people selling paper money. It was as if her last coin may vanish if she dared to even look at any of the vendors.

She ran through the gate and up the steps to the main temple hall. It was a small, simple building that had been painted yellow many years ago, but most of the paint had faded or peeled away. There was one small statue of Guanyin in the temple room, and only cushions for two people to pray on at a time, but more than that was only needed on festival days. She approached a monk and handed him the coin and her joss sticks.

"I know it isn't much," she said. "But it is all I have. Please pray for my mother so she will have a healthy son."

The monk smiled and took the coin. Then he lit her joss sticks and led her to the statue of Guanyin in the middle of the room.

Lihua placed the joss sticks into a long trough of ash that ran the length of the statue, then she kneeled on a red pillow in front of the display. The monk sat on a pillow next to her and recited a blessing as the two of them kowtowed to Guanyin three times. The monk gave her a smile and then went to help another petitioner. But Lihua lingered a little longer. She folded her hands in front of her and prayed as hard as she could for her mother and her little brother.

The thunder cracked and the wind howled as Lihua's mother labored with the baby through the night. The pregnancy had been difficult, with Mama always exhausted or ill. But that was over, and the baby would be here soon.

Lihua's father paced back and forth, and Nainai ran her fingers over the bodhi seeds of her bracelet at a furious pace. Lihua could not go outside and pray to the kitchen god over the doorway in the rain, so she kneeled just inside the open door and rocked nervously on her heels. All any of them could do was wait as two of their neighbors helped Mama bring her baby into the world.

"Lihua," Nainai called, waving her over. Nainai gripped Lihua's hands so tightly it was almost painful. "Whatever happens, you must be strong."

"I am sure Mama won't die," Lihua said.

"No, no," Nainai said, shaking her head.

"I'll be a good daughter," Lihua said. "And a good big sister."

"I know you will," Nainai said, her voice cracking. "I have never worried about you being good and doing the right thing. It's your mother—"

"Ma!" Lihua's father cut in. She looked at him and saw him sending a warning look to Nainai.

"What is it?" Lihua asked. "What about Mama?"

"Nothing," her father said. "Just...wait. It still might all be for nothing."

Lihua's brow furrowed. She didn't understand. In the months leading up to tonight, it was as if the family wanted the baby to die. In a way, she understood their fears. Many babies never arrived at all, and some were born sleeping.

Many did not live to see their first year. Not to mention that they were already barely scraping by. It was best to not get attached should the worst happen.

But Lihua couldn't think that way. She knew the goddess would protect the baby. Somehow, they would all find a way to survive—together.

The lightning struck and the wind blew the rain through the noodle shop. Lihua ran to the door to close it, but then she heard a voice behind her.

"The baby," the neighbor woman said, coming down the stairs.

Lihua, her father, and her grandmother all turned to the woman expectantly, holding their breaths.

"The baby has arrived alive," the woman said. "It is a boy."

Lihua exhaled with relief and a smile spread across her face. She looked to her father and grandmother, but they did not look at her, nor did they smile. They only looked at each other with grim faces.

"I warned you many years ago," her grandmother said to her father. "But you didn't listen." She spit on the ground, and Lihua gasped. Why would her grandmother be cursing her father on this joyous occasion?

Her father didn't reply. He only pressed his lips and then stomped upstairs, pushing past the neighbor woman. The other neighbor came down the stairs as well, holding a basin of bloody water and rags. She went to the door and tossed the water out into the street for the rain to wash away. Both of the women left the shop without a word to Lihua or Nainai.

"What is happening?" Lihua asked. "Why is no one happy?"

Nainai stood and cupped Lihua's chin in her hand. She

opened her mouth a few times to speak, but always shut it again. She finally shook her head and carefully climbed the stairs to her own room.

The doors banged open again. Lihua ran to push them closed, but as she looked out into the street, she gasped. A black and white shape quickly darted behind a house on the other side of the road and disappeared. She rubbed her eyes and looked again, but nothing was there.

She pondered over what it could have been. A dog? A spirit? A panda? A wisp of smoke? She almost laughed to herself. It was surely only her eyes playing tricks on her in the late, stormy night.

CHAPTER THREE

For the next couple of days, Lihua worked hard in the noodle shop so her mother could take time to relax and recuperate. She wasn't invited into her mother's room to see the new baby. But she could hear the baby crying and cooing and her mother talking to him, so she knew they were okay. She was anxious to see the baby, but she didn't ask to see him or her mother. She didn't want to be the cause of anyone's stress. She kept her head down, her voice quiet, and worked quickly and diligently.

The only thing that worried her were the harsh, low tones her mother, father, and grandmother used when speaking to each other behind the closed door. It seemed the three of them had not had a civil conversation since the baby was born. Lihua didn't know what they were fighting about, only that it was constant. She assumed they were talking about the future, how Mama was going to care for the restaurant and the baby at the same time. But she hoped that by doing a good job working the restaurant with Baba, Mama would see that she didn't need to worry.

Finally, early on the fourth morning, Mama came

downstairs, carrying the new baby wrapped tightly in a blanket.

Lihua was nearly bursting with excitement. She wanted to rush over and see the new baby, smell his hair, kiss his head. But she forced herself to remain calm and wait for her mother's instructions.

Baba brought an old wicker basket downstairs and placed it on a table. It had a blanket in the bottom for comfort and high sides to keep the baby from rolling out. Mama placed the baby in the basket, and then looked down at him and smiled. Baba placed a gentle hand on Mama's shoulder and looked down at the baby as well with love on his face.

Lihua's parents had never looked at her with such affection, and she felt a twinge of jealously in her chest. She did her best to shrug it away—all families were happier at the birth of a son than a daughter—but she felt the hurt just the same.

Still, Lihua felt a wave of anxiety roll off her shoulders at seeing Mama happy. Of course, Mama had been scared of the arrival of a new baby. What family wasn't worried about such a change? But he was here, and he was healthy. Everything would work out.

"Can I see him?" Lihua asked.

Mama and Baba straightened and looked at Lihua as though they had forgotten she was there.

Mama hesitated a moment, but then nodded. "Of course," she said. Lihua walked over and peeked in the basket at the baby.

He was perfect.

He was sleeping, but his mouth was slightly parted. His lips were plump and formed a perfect oval shape. His nose was short and broad but didn't take up too much of his face. His little fingers were pink and gently clasped together.

Lihua couldn't help but reach down and touch his hand and wrist. His skin was so soft it almost didn't feel real. Her heart swelled with love for this precious gift her family had been given and her eyes filled with tears.

Her finger nudged the edge of his sleeve, and something glinted beneath it. She moved the sleeve further out of the way and saw that he was wearing a silver bracelet. She shouldn't have been surprised—almost all new babies were given a silver bracelet to tie the baby to the world. But her family was so poor, she didn't expect him to have one. She didn't have one. Where did they get the money?

"Did you buy a bracelet for me when I was born?" Lihua asked. She wondered if her bracelet had been sold during a particularly dire time.

Her mother grimaced and turned away, mumbling, "I don't know."

Lihua felt a small bit of annoyance grumble in her stomach. What did she mean she didn't know?

"I have to start getting ready for the lunch crowd," her mother said.

"I can do that," Lihua said. "You rest, Mama."

"No, Lihua," Mama said. "You need to help Baba collect bamboo."

Lihua looked at her father, her brow scrunched. He had never needed her help before. Besides, girls didn't usually do outdoor work. Fathers and sons worked outside while mothers and daughters worked inside. Besides, hadn't she shown over the last few days that not only could she help in the shop, but she could run it on her own? Why would her mother suddenly send her to work with Baba?

"But, Mama, I—"

"Come on, Lihua," her father said as he collected his ropes and large bamboo hacking knife. "Let's go."

Lihua knew it was pointless and unfilial to argue, so she bit her tongue and followed Baba out of the village and into the bamboo forest.

She should have felt grateful to get out of the noisy, dirty, crowded city for half a day. And normally she would have been, but today...something was wrong. Why was everyone still upset. Why was she here in the woods and not at home? Where was Nainai?

The bamboo stalks creaked and clacked as they swayed back and forth. Baba moved to the thick grove and began hacking with his knife. She then realized that she didn't have a knife of her own. How was she supposed to help?

Baba hacked down a large stalk of bamboo, laid it along the ground, and began hacking it into smaller pieces. Lihua stood nearby, waiting for directions, but the directions never came. Baba then hacked down another stalk, and another, all the while never acknowledging her. Finally, Lihua had enough.

"Why am I here?" she asked, her arms folded over her chest.

Baba stopped mid-hack, his arm raised in the hair, his breathing labored, sweat pouring from his brow. He lowered his arm and looked at Lihua. He hesitated, but then he nodded.

"I have to tell you something, Lihua," he said. "I'm not your father."

Lihua's arms fell to her sides and her heart dropped into her stomach. "W-w-what?" she stammered.

"I'm not your father, Lihua," he repeated. "And Mama, she's not your mother."

Lihua's breath caught in her throat. Why was he saying this? It couldn't be true.

"We tried for many years to have a child," her father went on. "But it never happened. We saved money, every coin we could, and we finally bought you from a man who was passing through town with some children for sale. We wanted a boy, but they were too expensive, so we bought the youngest girl he had. You were that baby."

Lihua's head started to spin. Bought from a man...a man with many children for sale. Wanted a boy...wanted a boy... They always wanted a boy...

"W...was that man my father?" Lihua asked.

Baba...or whoever this man was, shook his head. "No," he said without further explanation.

A kidnapper. Or had she been sold? She had no idea. Who was she? Where had she come from? Her heart beat rapidly. She was going to be sick.

"Why are you telling me this?" she asked. She could have spent the rest of her life happily not knowing this. She loved her parents, her grandmother, her new baby brother...The baby! It was because of him.

Her father chewed on his lower lip for a moment before saying the words she knew were coming. "We cannot afford two children, Lihua."

A cry that Lihua had tried to keep silent in her chest finally burst forth. She ran from the forest and back toward the village. People stared as she flew past them, wailing as though she had been injured, but she didn't care. He was lying. He had to be. Her parents had always been cold and distant, but there were reasons for that. But her grandmother, she loved her. She would tell her the truth.

As she ran through the restaurant, her mother froze. It was as though she was shocked Lihua was there. But Lihua didn't stop to talk to her. She ran up the stairs and threw open the door to her room.

Her grandmother was kneeling before a small alter on a red cushion. The alter was painted with red lacquer. On top sat a serene Buddha in a lotus leaf. He was draped with prayer beads and three small oranges sat to one side as an offering. Joss sticks were slowly smoldering away in a holder in front of him. Other auspicious symbols were sitting haphazardly on the alter, but Lihua didn't look at them closely. She stood in the doorway panting, and her grandmother slowly turned to face her.

Nainai nodded sadly. "It's true," she said.

Lihua stumbled forward and collapsed into her grandmother's arms. Together, they wept.

"I told your parents it was a bad idea," Nainai said as she wiped Lihua's tears away when they both managed to finally stop crying. "To take in a child and not love it as your own, it was a wicked thing to do. But they didn't listen to me."

"They...they don't love me?" Lihua asked. She had always thought her parents were distant from her because they *did* love her. They were just steeling their hearts against the day she would leave them for her husband's home.

"Your father..." Nainai started to say, but then she stopped herself and shook her head. "I don't know. That man is not the boy I raised. But your mother, she has always been a cruel, cold-hearted thing. I told my husband, your grandfather, not to allow the match. But my voice didn't matter."

"And now?" Lihua asked. "Are you not the head of the family now?" As the oldest member of the family, all of the members were required to show her respect and listen to her voice. But Nainai shook her head sadly.

"My son is the man of the house," she said. "And now that your mother has a son, well...who am I but a worthless old woman?"

Lihua reached over and squeezed her hand. "I'll always honor you," she said.

"I wish I could do more for you, my pearl," Nainai said, more tears escaping down her face. "But your mother, she wants to sell you. She thinks we can at least get some money for the baby out of you."

"Sell me?" Lihua asked in horror. "To who?"

"It doesn't matter," Nainai said. "Your father, he wouldn't allow it. At least he did one good thing by you."

Lihua wasn't too sure about that. If her father were a good man, he wouldn't send her away at all. She still couldn't believe this was happening.

"So, what am I to do?" Lihua asked.

"I don't know," Nainai said. "By morning, your mother expects you to be gone. I'm sorry, my pearl."

"But...where do I go?" Lihua asked, panic rising up again. "Where am I from? Who will protect me?"

Nainai pulled Lihua down to her knees in front of the alter. "The ancestors will protect you."

Nainai reached up to the alter and pulled down a silver bracelet. She tried to force the bracelet around Lihua's hand, but the bracelet was too small. Lihua looked closely, hoping the bracelet held a clue, but some of the etching had worn away and many characters she didn't recognize at all.

"The baby seller," Nainai said. "He said he got you from

Changsha, in Hunan, to the east of the Dayong Mountains. You were wearing this bracelet."

Her missing birth bracelet! Her parents—her birth parents—must have given this to her as a baby. They had loved her that much at least. And Nainai had kept it all these years.

"Do you think I should go to Changsha?" Lihua asked. "Will I find my parents there?" She had never even heard of this place, or Hunan, before. She knew nothing outside of her village and the bamboo forest beyond it. She had heard many people speak of the Dayong Mountains, but she had never seen them.

"I do not know where your path will lead you, my pearl," Nainai said. "But if we pray to the ancestors, they will guide and protect you."

Nainai lit a new joss stick and placed it in front of the Buddha. She then began to kowtow and pray. But Lihua shook her head.

"Nainai," Lihua said. "Whose ancestors are you praying to? Yours or mine?"

Nainai froze for a moment. Ancestor worship was an intimate part of life, yet Lihua had spent her whole life praying to people she wasn't related to. Would they still protect her? Or would they ignore her pleas? If her own parents had abandoned her, why would people who lived and died before she was even born care about her?

Nainai opened the door to the alter and pulled out a large bag of joss sticks. She also pulled out a small bag of coins. She handed both items to Lihua.

"Every temple you pass, light some incense and say a prayer, just in case," Nainai said.

Lihua squeezed her grandmother's hand one last time and then went to her bed. She pulled out a small bag and put her few clothing items, the joss sticks, a box of matches, and the bag of coins into it.

She took a deep breath and went downstairs. The restaurant was full of people now. They were all talking and laughing and eating and barely noticed her. Her mother was busy serving bowls of noodles, but she froze when Lihua entered the room.

Lihua's heart went cold. She went to the jar of huajiao and poured a sizeable amount into a small cloth and tied them securely before putting them into her bag as well.

She started to walk out when she saw the basket that held her baby brother. She went to him and looked down. His eyes were open and he was smiling up at her. His black eyes shined and his cheeks dimpled. Her heart melted a little and she couldn't help but smile back. She reached down and stroked his rosy face.

"Goodbye, little brother," she said. "Good luck. In this family, you'll need it."

She straightened up, put her bag over her shoulder, and walked out of the restaurant.

"Hey, Lihua!" one of the customers called out. "Where are you going?"

She didn't respond. She didn't say goodbye to her mother. She didn't look for her father. She realized that she never learned her baby brother's name, but she didn't see the point in asking now.

She knew she would never again see the only family she had ever known.

CHAPTER FOUR

As Lihua walked toward the edge of town, she realized she hadn't taken any food with her, but she refused to go back. She stopped at a baozi shop and used some of the coins her grandmother had given her to buy some steamed buns for the road, wrapping them in a cloth and putting them into her bag, which was slung across her back.

There was only one road that ran east to west through her town. She stopped to consider which way to go but quickly realized it didn't matter. She recalled the popular phrase, "East or west, home is best," but she didn't have a home. She didn't have a family. She had no job, no responsibilities, and no hope for the future. She didn't even know if she would be able to find food the next day. Where would she sleep that night?

She placed her hand on her chest as her heart started to race. She couldn't stop herself from looking back toward her parents' noodle shop. She couldn't see it from where she was standing, but she had hoped to maybe see her mother or father coming after her. How could they just send her away like that? Even if she was adopted, they were they only parents she knew. They had raised her and cared for her. She was a Bashu girl, a spicy girl. This was her home.

And yet, it wasn't. She had always thought her parents' treatment of her had been because she was a girl. Now she knew it was because they never loved her. Never considered her to be their own child. As soon as Mama gave birth to a new child, she was cast aside. If the baby had been a girl, would they have still sent her away? She imagined it was likely. A girl would be helpless, useless, but it would at least be *their* little girl. Lihua was a stranger.

Lihua turned back to the road. Her parents weren't coming. That part of her life was over. She had to decide—east or west.

The only thing she knew about life outside her village was that the Dayong Mountains were to the east. She had been told they were so tall, they reached up to the sky and practically floated among the clouds. She could hardly imagine such a thing, so she needed to see them for herself. She turned to the right and headed east.

As Lihua started walking along the rough and dirty road, she tried to understand how she came to be in this situation. What had she done wrong? She had tried to work hard, be filial and dutiful. She prayed to the ancestors and Guanyin. She did like to eat, though. A new baby would only drink milk for a long time. And she often ran off with the other children and played in the woods. She should have worked harder and played less. If she ever found a new family, she would be more like her mother and never stop working.

A new family? Should she look for a new family? She was only twelve. Most girls didn't marry out until they were fourteen, or even sixteen. She was still a child, and she was small for her age. People often thought she appeared younger than she was. Maybe if a family bought her once, she could find an adoptive family a second time.

No, there was no hope in dreaming of that. Who would want a girl her age? One about to be old enough to marry out anyway. Besides, no one wanted girls. Everyone wanted a boy.

Is that why her birth family got rid of her too? Her heart felt heavy at the thought. She was so worthless, tossed aside by one family after another just because she was a girl. Maybe she should pretend to be a boy. She could cut her hair and change her name. No one would know...well, for a while anyway. She knew that boys were different from girls. When she had been little, all the girls and boys from the village would swim naked in the river to cool off. She would be found out eventually.

She thought about the man her parents bought her from. Her grandmother had said he had many children for sale. Where did he get them? Where did he get her? Did he kidnap her? Steal her from her basket at night? It was possible. If her adoptive parents couldn't have children and were so desperate they would buy a child, there must be many people in the world willing to do the same thing. How many children had been stolen from their parents and sold over the years? Those parents must have been so devastated to lose their children. Did her parents still think about her? Did they miss her?

She sat on a rock on the side of the road to rest her feet. They were already getting tired. But as she looked back in the direction she came from, she didn't think she had walked very far. She could still see smoke and dust rising from the village over the trees in the distance. How far were the mountains? How many days would it take to get there? How many nights? She pulled one of the baozi out of her bag and ate it. How long would her food last?

She looked up at the sky and saw that it was only early afternoon. By now, back at her parents' noodle shop, the mid-day meal rush would be over and everyone would be lying down for a well-earned rest. Well, not everyone. Lihua had always had plenty of energy. She would often use the break to find the other children and go play in the forest. And not her mother. She would find something to do. Washing, preparing vegetables or noodles, mending old clothes. Lihua wished she had spent more time helping her mother with the chores.

She grunted as she stuffed the last bite of steamed bun into her mouth and stood back up, forcing herself to keep going. She had to stop thinking about her family. They didn't want her. And it didn't matter how far away the mountains were, she didn't have anywhere else to go. A day, a month, a year. She had to keep walking.

And she couldn't dwell on her birth family either. She could never find them. Where was Changsha? She had no idea. Further away than the mountains, that much she knew. But there must be millions of people in the world. How would she ever find two people she never met? She didn't know their names. She didn't even know her own name. She wasn't even sure she had been kidnapped. Her parents could have simply sold her to that child seller. How else could he have so many children? If he were kidnapping children, someone would have stopped him, right? She was a worthless girl. It made sense that her family had sold her. Especially if they had a son later. Isn't that what Nainai had said Mama wanted to do? Sell her to someone now that she had a son. Maybe that was what her birth mother did too.

Maybe this was something parents did with children they didn't want. She thought back to all the times women in the village were known to be pregnant—the signs were always easy enough to spot—and then suddenly they would no longer be pregnant, but they wouldn't have a baby either. Lihua had always assumed the baby died, but what if something much worse was happening. Something Lihua had been too young and blind to see. Something terrible. Cruel, selfish parents selling off the children they didn't want. Children who didn't ask to be brought into this world. Children like her, passed from family to family, never knowing who they were, where they were from, or where they were going.

Lihua's feet were getting heavy and her legs sore. But she screwed up her face, tied her bag tighter on her back, and pushed herself to keep going. She had to forget. She had to keep going. She had to survive.

She would find a new place in this world all by herself.

CHAPTER FIVE

As she passed through another village, she asked a woman if she was going the right way to the Dayong Mountains, and she said she was. Lihua then asked if there was a temple in the village, and she was pointed down a short street.

She was struck by how much the village looked like her own. She had never been to another village before, and she wasn't sure why she had expected anything different. She wondered if the whole world looked like her hometown—just a bunch of small villages stretching endlessly. People going about their daily lives, cooking, cleaning, eating, farming, praying, just trying to make it from one day to the next. It suddenly all sounded very pointless to her, but what else could she do?

She went through the temple gate and lit one of her joss sticks on an open flame in the middle of the courtyard. The joss stick sparked and sputtered, and she blew the flame out quickly, setting it to its slow, fragrant burn.

Instead of going into the main temple where the shrine

to the local god would be, she went to a side building, where the village's ancestor tablets were stored.

Most families knew their lineage for several generations back, but often whole villages could trace their roots to a common ancestor. The whole village would pray to these ancestors for protection and guidance.

Lihua placed her joss stick in the offering trough and then kneeled and performed a kowtow. Then she sat up and prayed out loud with her hands folded in front of her.

"I know my offering is small, but I have a long journey ahead, and many more temples to visit," she said. "I know it is very unlikely that I came from this village. But even if you are not my ancestors, would you look out for me? Just until I find out where I belong?" She then kowtowed three times again.

She doubted the ancestors heard her. After all, she was just one little nobody and they had a whole village of their own descendants to protect, but maybe, just maybe, one of the ancestors would hear her plea.

It was getting late in the day and she was sore from head to toe, but feeling encouraged after her prayer and knowing she was heading in the right direction, she decided to press onward. She didn't know anyone in the village and wouldn't be able to afford a room anyway. Eventually, when she grew tired enough, she would just have to find a place along the road to sleep. She hoped the night wouldn't get too cold.

As she walked along the road, she passed various people throughout the day. Most of them were traveling from their farms in the countryside to sell their vegetables or chickens in the villages while some were moving their cows from stream to grazing land and back again. So when she heard three men walk up behind her, she didn't think anything of it at first.

"Where are you going, little girl?" the first man, a tall skinny fellow, asked as he walked up next to her.

"Dayong," she said with a smile. "I'm going to see the mountains."

"All by yourself?" a second man, this one with very bad teeth, asked her. He and the third man were walking behind her.

The smile instinctively ran from her face as alarms starting going off in her head. She shook her head and averted her eyes.

"No," she said. "My baba is in the next village."

The third man mumbled something in an accent so grating on the ears, she couldn't understand what he said.

"What?" she asked.

"He asked how far the next village was," the first man translated.

"Oh," she said, tightening her grip on the strap to her bag and stepping closer to the edge of the road. "It is very near. Just...just over that ridge." She looked up the road to a slight rise and hoped she was right. But she had just left a village not long ago, so she hadn't planned on seeing another village tonight.

"What a coincidence," the man said. "That's where we're going. Why don't we walk together?"

Lihua felt her heart beat so fast she thought it would burst right out of her chest. She gripped the strap on her bag so tightly, her knuckles were white. But she smiled and nodded and prayed that there was something, anything—a village, a farm, even a kindly old man in a remote field would be better than nothing.

She looked to the right, into the bamboo forest. If she needed to run, that would be her only chance of escape. There was no way she could hope to fight off three men. If they managed to grab her, that would be it. She didn't see any ropes or weapons, but they wouldn't need them to subdue her.

As they walked up the hill, her mouth went completely dry, and she licked her lips constantly. Her heart beat so hard she could hear the blood whooshing in her ears. As they reached the top of the rise, her body erupted into a full panic.

"Well, what do you know," the first man said. "No village."

Before he even stopped speaking, Lihua took off at a run into the forest.

"Get her!" she heard one of the other men say, which was unnecessary because she could hear all three of them already chasing after her.

She didn't look ahead to see where she was going, she simply held her hands in front of her to move any leaves or branches out of her way.

"Stop, little girl!" one of the men yelled. "We aren't going to hurt you."

Her gut told her otherwise. If her own parents could abandon her, she was sure these strange men were capable of much worse.

"Gotcha!" one of the men yelled as he grabbed her hair, which had been plaited down her back.

She didn't think, she only reacted. She turned and kicked him in the leg as hard as she could. It wasn't particularly hard, but he let her go anyway with a grunt. She thought she must have only surprised him, but she didn't dwell on it. She turned and ran again, this time darting left and right. She didn't bother screaming. No one would hear her; and if they did, no one would come to her aid. She was all alone in the woods. She needed to get away, needed to hide.

After a moment, she didn't hear the footsteps behind her anymore, but she could still hear noises, voices. She dropped to her knees behind a tree and listened.

"You go that way; I'll go this way," someone said.

She had escaped for now, but they hadn't given up. She took a deep breath and then slapped her hand over her mouth. She needed to be quiet. If they lost sight of her for long enough, maybe they would go away.

She listened to their footsteps as they split up and went in different directions. The steps got quieter and quieter, until they eventually stopped altogether. She waited what felt like ages before getting up the courage to peek around the side of the tree. She was shaking, but as she looked around, she saw nothing. She sighed as she sat back down and leaned against the tree. She closed her eyes and thanked the ancestors for protecting her.

"Found you!" one of the men yelled as he jumped in front of her.

This time, she did scream. He leaned down to grab her, but she scurried between his legs and took off at a run again. She heard him let out a curse as he turned to chase after her.

She was exhausted and crying. She darted from side to side in the unfamiliar forest. She had no idea which way to go and was scared she was going to run right into one of the other men. The forest was darkening, both from growing thicker and from the setting sun. She could barely see where she was going, but she kept running.

Her heart beat painfully hard in her chest. She wasn't going to last much longer. Her first day on her own and she was going to be killed. What an end to a short and miserable life.

She smacked into something furry, warm, and hard, causing her to fall backward and knock the wind out of her chest. As she looked back at what she had run in to, her eyes widened. It was a large, lumbering creature. She watched as the beast turned to face her, revealing a white band around its stomach, chest, and face. Then the creature reared up on its hind legs and roared.

A giant panda!

She had never seen one in person, and it was much larger and more frightening than she expected. She gasped as it roared and quivered as it swiped one of its clawed paws over her.

She screamed as she cowered, covering her head with her arms.

She was done for.

CHAPTER SIX

"Get back, beast!" Lihua heard one of the men yell.

The panda dropped to her forelegs over Lihua and growled at the would-be attacker.

The man grabbed a large stick off the ground and swung it at the panda. The panda stepped over Lihua toward the man, grabbing the stick with her powerful jaw and ripping it from his grasp. The panda then lunged forward, biting him on the leg. The man fell to the ground screaming.

One of the other men came upon the scene and cursed. He picked up a stone and threw it at the panda. The panda released the man from her jaw and ran toward the second man. The second man ran away, nearly knocking the third man over in his haste to escape. The man who was injured used the distraction to hobble away.

The panda did not pursue the men, but let out a satisfied huff once their screams were out of earshot. Then the panda turned back to Lihua.

Lihua hadn't moved from her spot on the ground, too shocked by what she had seen to move. She had never seen a panda before and had no idea how dangerous they could be. She now realized that she should have run away while the panda was attacking the men, but it was too late.

She and the panda locked eyes.

The panda ambled toward her, and Lihua once again hid her face in her arms. She then felt a warm breeze on the back of her neck as the panda sniffed her hair. The panda let out a grunt as she sat back on her haunches.

Lihua slowly lifted her head. The panda just sat there, looking at her curiously. Lihua crawled backward, and the panda did not react other than to tilt her head to the side. Lihua scooted behind a tree and took a deep breath. It was as though she had not taken a breath from the moment she first saw the panda. She leaned against the tree and breathed in and out several times, filling her lungs to keep from passing out. When she finally calmed down, she peeked back around the tree.

The panda was gone.

She exhaled a sigh of relief, thinking the panda must have gotten bored and wandered away. But as she turned back to her spot behind the tree, she found herself nose to nose with the big black and white face of the bear. Lihua gasped in terror as she fell back away from the panda.

"N-n-nice panda," Lihua finally muttered, holding her hand out in front of her. "Please don't hurt me."

The panda stepped forward and sniffed Lihua's hand. Then she stuck out her tongue and licked it.

Lihua pulled her hand, now warm and wet from the panda's tongue, back and scooted away. The panda did not follow, but sat back once again and looked at her. Lihua forced herself to her feet and backed away.

"I'm going now," Lihua said. "Don't follow me."

The panda cocked her head back and forth but didn't get up.

Lihua backed up a few more steps and then looked around. She had no idea where she was. The forest was thick here, and the sun had nearly set. She was completely turned around and had no idea how to get back to the road. Of course, she wasn't sure she even wanted to go back to the road. If those men found her again, who knew what they would do to her. And there could be other bad men on the road as well.

But she didn't want to go deeper into the woods either. Pandas weren't the only dangerous animals out there. Her grandmother had told her about all kinds of vicious beasts —tigers, wolves, ancient monsters with large horns. Not to mention trickster fairies. And what if she fell in a hole or tripped and broke her leg. No one would ever find her out here.

Her eyes started to water as the hopelessness of her plight washed over her. She was a child alone in the woods... Alone in the world. She had no one to protect her. She didn't even know where she was going to spend the night if she did find the road.

She felt the warm, wet breath of the panda on her hand. She instinctively jerked her hand away, but when she looked down, she didn't see a monstrous beast. The panda looked up at her with big, kind eyes and nuzzled her hip.

Cautiously, Lihua lowered her hand, letting the panda sniff it again. The panda snuffled her, and then maneuvered her head under Lihua's hand. Lihua laid her hand on the panda's head and then started to pet her.

Her fur was thick and soft, and Lihua's hand could get completely buried in it. As she ran her hand over the luscious fur, she felt calm once again.

The panda then started to walk away.

"Wait," Lihua said. "Where are you going?"

The panda looked at her and grunted, then kept walking. With nowhere else to go, Lihua followed the panda.

The panda wandered deeper into the woods at a slow, ambling pace, as though she had nowhere important to be. Lihua supposed she didn't. She began to think that the life of a panda, or any animal, would be far less stressful than that of a human. All animals needed to worry about was sleeping and eating. They could live outdoors and eat plants. They didn't need to worry about clothes to wear or if they had any friends. And the babies grew up fast, often leaving their parents and starting their own families within a year, according to what she remembered from seeing the many cats and dogs around her village. She wished she had been big enough to leave her family years ago, or was even big enough to be on her own now. Even though she ran away, she knew she couldn't survive on her own for long. Eventually, she would need to find a new family, or at least a new village. A place where she could find work and a safe place to sleep.

She had been so deep in her own thoughts, she was surprised when she and the panda came upon a stream. She hadn't realized how thirsty she was. She had packed some food, but she had no way to carry any water with her. The panda dipped her head down and lapped up the water. Lihua kneeled down next to her and used her hands to cup the water and bring it to her mouth. It was cool and clean and just what she needed. When she drank her fill, she sat back on her heels and watched as the panda continued to gulp the water. She knew it was crazy, but she couldn't help but wonder if the panda somehow knew what she needed.

When the panda finally had enough to drink, she led

Lihua back into the forest. They walked for quite a while, and Lihua was beginning to wonder if the panda had no particular goal in mind when they finally came to a small clearing. The grass had been padded down and extra leaves and branches had been added to the area. Lihua realized it was a sort of panda nest, a place where the panda had probably been living for some months. She then looked in the middle of the nest and saw a small black and white mound of fluffy fur. A baby panda!

"You're a mama!" Lihua exclaimed as the panda went and curled up next to the baby. But then Lihua noticed that the baby didn't move or make a sound even when the mama panda nudged it with her nose.

"I'm so sorry," Lihua said when she realized that the baby panda was dead. The mama panda looked at her and then let out a long sigh as she laid her head down to rest.

Lihua sat down at the edge of the nest and leaned against a tree. She felt an overwhelming sadness come over her as she looked at the mama panda snuggling her baby.

"At least there is one good mother left in this world," she whispered. She said a small prayer to Guanyin, asking that in her next life she be born a panda.

She reached into her bag and pulled out one of her baozi. She wasn't exactly hungry, but it had been a long and exhausting day and she knew she needed to eat. She forced the steamed bun with a meaty center down her throat as the sun completely set, enveloping the forest in darkness.

She sat for a long time, listening as the forest seemed to come more alive at night. Bugs chirped, the bamboo trees creaked, and every once in a while, she was sure she heard a low growl or moan from some unknown animal prowling nearby.

But the mama panda didn't seem a bit concerned as she

laid curled up in the middle of the nest, her body rising and lowering as she took deep, steady breaths.

Lihua knew she was safe here. If the panda wasn't scared, then she had no reason to be. She finally piled some leaves up into a pillow and laid her head down, even though she couldn't imagine she would get any sleep. Her mind continued to race over everything that had brought her to this moment and every possible path her life could take going forward.

She felt a knot in her stomach tighten and twist as she tried to rest but only thought about how her parents so callously pushed her out of their lives. She didn't want to think about it, but she couldn't stop herself. How could they? Could she have done anything to change their minds? What about Nainai? She was so sure Nainai loved her. Couldn't she have done more to protect her? She had been gone a whole day. Did they miss her now that she was gone? Maybe she should go back. Maybe they would take her back into their arms and tell her how wrong and sorry they were.

Her heart sank even further into despair. Her mother had never embraced her even in the best of times. Why would she welcome her into her arms now? No, that was not her mother's way.

Finally, out of sheer exhaustion and heartache, Lihua began to cry. She didn't want to. What good would it do? But she couldn't stop herself. She was alone. She was scared. She was hungry. She was lost. If she simply died, no one would mourn her or miss her. No one would light incense for her or have an ancestor stone carved for her. Even death would not be a release. She would be forced to walk the earth as a hungry ghost for eternity.

She felt a warm, furry mass lay down next to her. She rolled over and realized that the mama panda had left the center of the nest—and her baby—and had curled up next to her instead. She couldn't explain it, but she felt instantly better. She snuggled up next to the panda and found her heat and heartbeat soothing. In no time at all, Lihua fell asleep.

CHAPTER SEVEN

The sun was shining and the birds were chirping when Lihua woke up the next morning with the panda still by her side. She felt rested and ready to face the day. The complete despair she had felt enveloping her the night before had lifted somewhat. She still felt the gnawing pain of sadness deep in heart, but—for the moment at least—it was not consuming her.

It was not until she sat up and stretched that the panda too got up from her sleeping spot. The panda then wandered over to a bamboo stalk and easily pulled it down, ripping into it with her claws to get at the tender bamboo meat inside. Lihua took out another steamed bun from her bag and ate it, lamenting over how the buns were already starting to turn bad. She would have to find more food again soon. She was also thirsty. She wondered if she would be able to find her way back to the stream.

When she finally finished eating, she knew there was no reason to linger. She stood up, dusted herself off, and put her bag back over her shoulder.

"Thank you, panda," she said as the bear lazily chewed

on the now empty stalks. "I can never repay you for saving me from those men and keeping me safe through the night, but I need to be going now."

When she stepped out of the nest, the panda grunted at her. She waved goodbye and started to walk away, but the panda followed her. As she stopped and looked back, the panda let out what could only be described as a whimper as she looked back at the nest, and then to Lihua.

"What's wrong?" Lihua asked, even though she knew the panda couldn't answer.

The panda grunted again and shifted from one foot to another anxiously.

Lihua took a step back toward the panda, and the panda retreated back to the nest. Lihua went back and saw that the mama panda was pacing around the baby.

"Oh," Lihua said. "I see." The panda wanted to follow her but didn't want to leave her baby behind. Lihua kneeled down by the mama panda and her baby. "We need to bury it."

Lihua reached down and wrapped the little bundle of fur in a large leaf. The mama panda followed Lihua's every movement with her nose. Lihua then moved the leaves and grass from the nest to the side and dug a hole in the dirt with her hands. She then placed the baby panda in the hole and gently covered her with the dirt, grass, and leaves. The mama panda laid by the hole and whimpered as her baby disappeared.

"She will be safe here," Lihua whispered. She then reached into her bag and pulled out a joss stick and match. She lit the incense and stuck it into the ground next to where the baby was buried. She closed her eyes and folded her hands in front of her.

"Dear Goddess of Mercy," Lihua prayed. "Please watch

over and protect this little panda on her journey and help her as she travels to the next life. Please help her find her mama again." She then kowtowed three times. She reached out and petted the mama panda on the head. "She's in a better place now."

The panda let out a sad grunt as she and Lihua stood up and walked out of the nest.

"You don't have to follow me," Lihua said. "Where I'm going, I don't think a panda can follow anyway. Not that I know where I'm going, but I am sure I will find a village or even a city eventually. A panda can't live in a city."

The panda groaned but kept following. Lihua sighed. It wasn't like she could tell a panda what to do. And traveling with a panda was at least better than traveling alone. The panda had saved her from those bad men and showed her where the stream was. The panda would know more about surviving in the woods than she did.

"Okay, fine," Lihua finally said to the panda. "You can come with me, at least for now. Have you ever been to the mountains...Umm...Hmm. I think you need a name."

The panda didn't respond, but continued following Lihua dutifully.

"I've never met a panda before," Lihua said. She momentarily considered how silly it was that she was talking to a panda, but she knew many of her friends who talked to their pets. She never had a pet herself. Pets would have cost money, or at least extra food they didn't have. But she always enjoyed playing with the cats and dogs and even small monkeys some of the other village children kept as pets. "What is a good name for a panda?"

The panda snuffled at a fern, biting off some leaves.

"How about Maomao?" Lihua asked, since one of the

characters that made up the word "panda" was the same as "cat."

The panda then spit out some of the fern leaves, evidently deciding they weren't very delicious.

"Actually, you don't really look like a cat to me," Lihua said. "What about Heihei, since your fur is black?"

The panda let out an annoyed grunt.

"Though I suppose you are as white as you are black," Lihua said with a sigh as she broke a small twig off of a tree and started to chew on it to distract herself from her growing hunger.

"How about Panpan?" Lihua finally asked. "I don't think it means anything, but it's cute."

Panpan let out a small grunt that sounded like an agreement to Lihua.

"Panpan it is," Lihua said, feeling oddly triumphant over this decision. "So, Panpan, have you ever been to the Dayong Mountains? That's where I'm going."

Panpan didn't reply as they started to climb up the side of a hill.

Lihua huffed and puffed a little. "We will need to work on our mountain climbing skills before we get there."

They got to the top of the hill and saw a stream running below them. Lihua had no idea if this was the same stream from the day before, but it was wider here, practically a river, and there were several women there washing clothes. They had some children with them as well.

Lihua crouched down to hide, and Panpan sat down as well. Lihua wasn't sure why she felt afraid, but after her incident with the men on the road, she thought it was probably better to be cautious.

The women laughed and talked as they worked, and their

children splashed in the water. She then noticed that the women all had small lidded jars with them. She realized one of the jars would be perfect for carrying water in, something she desperately needed. She had a few coins in her bag that Nainai had given her. Hopefully it would be enough to buy a water jar.

"Panpan," Lihua whispered. "Stay here. I'm going to go down there. I'll be right back."

Panpan grunted anxiously as Lihua stood up.

"Shh!" Lihua said, trying to calm Panpan. "You have to be quiet." She stepped over the ridge and started to descend the side of the hill. Unfortunately, Panpan started to go with her. "No!" Lihua tried to whisper harshly, but it came out much louder than she expected. Panpan started to lumber down the hillside.

Lihua pushed against Panpan, trying to stop her, but Panpan was heavy and solid. Lihua's foot slipped and she found herself rolling down the hill, with a worried Panpan following after her. When Lihua finally stopped her descent, she heard some screams from below.

"A panda! Run!" someone yelled.

"It's killing that girl!" another woman exclaimed.

"No!" Lihua called out. "I'm fine!" But it was too late. The women were frantic, grabbing their children and running along the river and into the woods, presumably back to their village.

Panpan continued her way down the hill toward the river.

"Stop!" Lihua called out, but she supposed it didn't matter now, so she gave up and ran down to the river as well. "Fine," she said as Panpan started drinking from the water. "But we have to hurry. They will probably send men from the village back here."

She kneeled down to get a drink, but she noticed that

several of the women had left their washing supplies behind, including soap, clothes, and the water jars. She knew it was wrong, but she grabbed a jar and a bar of soap. She could have used the clothes as well, but they were all sopping wet, so she left them behind. She filled one of the jars with water and then headed back up the hill into the woods, calling for Panpan to follow her.

"We need to get out of here," she said. Just as they crested the hill, she heard voices from below. She looked down river and saw several men with farming tools marching toward where the women had been working. She crouched down and motioned for Panpan to do the same. She thought they would make less noise if they stayed still than if they tried to run away. Thankfully, Panpan sat down next to her and didn't make a sound.

She peeked over the hill and watched as the men surveyed the area. They didn't seem too keen to go into the woods looking for the panda or the girl it supposedly mauled. They walked along the hillside, looking for anything suspicious, but eventually they seemed satisfied at finding nothing. They gathered up the things the women left behind and headed back to their village.

Lihua breathed a sigh of relief. "That was close," she said. "We have to be careful. Humans are scared of pandas. And sometimes, humans kill them and sell their fur for lots of money."

Panpan raised her head at this.

"You don't need to worry," Lihua said. "As long as we avoid people, we will both be safe. Come on." She stood up, put her soap and water jar in her bag, and began walking again.

At this point, she had no idea if she was headed in the right direction or not. For all she knew, she could be heading back toward her home village. But she didn't know what else to do. At least she wasn't alone, as Panpan continued to follow.

She knew her advice to avoid people was best. Both a young girl and a panda could be stolen and sold for money. But as her stomach growled, she didn't know for how much longer she would be able to hide in the woods.

CHAPTER EIGHT

That night, as Lihua and Panpan curled up to go to sleep, Lihua ate her last baozi. It tasted terrible, but it was all she had. She was glad she had the clean river water to wash it down with, but soon that was gone as well. She had no idea how she was going to survive the next day.

In the morning, they started walking again and soon came upon a road. Lihua was relieved, but she and Panpan continued traveling through the forest where they could see the road but people traveling the road would not be able to see them. They did not see many people for most of the day, but the road got busier the further they went, so Lihua knew they had to be getting close to a village.

Lihua could smell the small community before she could see it. It was early evening, and people were cooking supper in their homes and shops. Her stomach rumbled violently as she had only had twigs to chew on all day.

"Roast meat!" a man on the edge of town called out. He didn't even have a shop, just a small portable grill he used to cook meat and vegetables on sticks.

Lihua eyed his wares hungrily, her mouth watering. She

licked her lips and tried to decide what to do. The money in her pouch wouldn't buy her much, but it would at least get her something. She just had to find ways to make it through each day, and today she needed to buy some of that grilled food on sticks.

"Panpan," she said as she crouched down in the bushes outside of town. "I need you to stay here, okay? You can still see me, but you can't follow me."

Panpan grunted and nudged Lihua with her nose. Lihua had a bad feeling that Panpan wasn't going to let her out of her sight, but she had to get the food.

Lihua held her hands in front of her as she backed away toward the village. "Stay," she whispered, but she didn't stand a chance at telling Panpan what to do. As she got to the edge of the village, Panpan walked right into the town as though she had no reason to fear the humans living there.

Several people who saw Panpan ran away in terror. The man who was running the grill, though, refused to leave his stall. He picked up a stick and held it like a weapon.

"Get back, monster!" he yelled as Panpan sniffed at the food.

"She's not a monster," Lihua tried to explain as she glanced around. Thankfully, most of the people had fled or were watching from a distance. "She's my friend. Can I buy some food?" she asked, hoping she could purchase some food and get back into the forest before any men with real weapons showed up.

The man looked at her like she was crazy. "What? Get out of here!" he yelled.

Panpan growled and began butting the grill with her head.

"Panpan! Stop!" Lihua cried, but it was too late. Much of

the food fell from the grill and onto the ground. Panpan chomped on some of the meat even though it was dirty.

"What's going on here?" another man asked, coming up behind her.

Lihua looked back and saw that a crowd was gathering around. Her eyes started to water.

"Please, I'm sorry," she said. "I'm just hungry. I wanted to buy some food."

"That panda just cost me all my food for the night!" the meat seller said. "You think you have that much money?"

"I...I don't know," Lihua said, wiping tears from her eyes.

"Why don't you sell me that panda instead then?" the man said.

"What?" Lihua asked.

"You said this is your panda?" he asked. "I'll take it and we can call it even."

Lihua looked around at the angry and confused faces and the dirty food on the ground. She was hungry and scared. She couldn't give up Panpan, but her stomach growled so loudly she was sure the people around her could hear it.

"No," Lihua said, pulling out her pitiful coin purse. "This is all I have. You can have it. Just...just give me some of the dirty food and we will go."

The people were now murmuring around her, and she could feel the tension growing.

"A panda skin could feed the whole village for a month," she heard one of the women say, and several people agreed with her.

Lihua knew it was time to go. She kneeled down and grabbed several of the food sticks and handed the coins to the seller.

"This isn't enough!" he said, grabbing her arm. "Maybe I'll take you in payment."

"Let me go!" Lihua cried as she struggled to free herself. As soon as her voice rang out, she heard Panpan growl. The vendor let go of Lihua's arm as Panpan lunged for him.

The people watching suddenly broke out in a panic again, running and screaming. Lihua put herself in Panpan's path to keep her from mauling the man.

"Panpan, stop!" she said. "Let's go!" She ran toward the woods, and Panpan followed right on her heels. She was afraid the village men would follow them, so even after they entered the forest, she kept running. She and Panpan ran as far and as fast as they could, not stopping even after they could no longer hear or smell the village behind them. Lihua finally only stopped running when they came to a stream. Even then, she crossed over it and followed it for quite a distance before she finally stopped to rest.

Somehow, she had managed to keep a grip on the sticks of food, but they were caked with dirt. She kneeled down by the river, and as she used the cold water to wash the dirt from the food, she began to weep.

How did this happen? Only a week before, she was safe in her own home with a loving grandmother and a baby brother on the way. Now, she was starving in the woods washing dirt off of sticks of scrawny meat she had practically stolen to survive.

She wasn't even hungry enough to eat anymore. She sat the food on the ground next to her and buried her head in her knees as she cried. She began to wonder if letting her mother sell her to another family would have been better. At least she would have had a roof over her head and clean food to eat. But even if she wanted to return to her village, she had no idea how to get back. She didn't know where she was. Had she walked hundreds of li toward the Dayong Mountains? Or was she only wandering in circles one hill over?

Panpan crouched next to her and nudged the food in Lihua's direction. Lihua picked it up and pulled some of the meat off the stick, forcing it in her mouth. It was damp and stringy, but as she looked at Panpan's deep eyes, she forced herself to swallow.

"It would be better if you left me here, Panpan," Lihua said. "I would hate for you to have to bury another child." Even though she wasn't going to die here in this moment, she didn't see a reason to keep going. It would be easier to lie down and not get up again. Maybe she would get lucky and die in her sleep.

Panpan grunted as she stood up. She pushed at Lihua with her nose, urging her into the woods. Once they were in a secluded area, Panpan walked in a circle, stamping down the grass and twigs, making a little nest in which to rest. She then laid down and grunted at Lihua again. Lihua obeyed and curled up next to the giant panda. Once again safe against Panpan's warm body and soothed by her steady heartbeat, Lihua fell asleep.

The next morning, as sunlight filtered through the trees and shined down on Lihua's face and the birds chirped, she rolled onto her back to discover that Panpan was not there. She sighed as a tear escaped her eye and rolled down her cheek. Now she was truly alone. She instantly regretted telling Panpan that she should leave. She hadn't thought her life could get much worse, but the emptiness she felt at having been abandoned by her panda was far more painful than she could have imagined.

A crashing sound behind her made her sit up.

"Panpan!" she cried as she saw the panda dragging a long bamboo stalk toward her. She jumped up and ran to Panpan, throwing her arms around the panda's neck. "I'm so glad you didn't listen to me! I'm sorry. Please don't ever leave me!"

Panpan dropped the bamboo and then licked Lihua's face. Lihua used the back of her hand to wipe the slobber away.

"Are you hungry?" Lihua asked as she looked at the bamboo stalk.

Panpan used her powerful jaws and claws to rip the bamboo stalk open, then she pushed it toward Lihua.

Lihua chuckled. "That's very sweet, Panpan," she said. "But I'm not a panda. I can't eat raw bamboo. It's poison. It would have to be cooked, like in a hotpot or over a..." She then remembered how her father would cook the bamboo in the stalk over the fire at their noodle shop. "Over a fire!"

Lihua picked up a bamboo stalk that Panpan had split open and went down to the river. The river's edge was rocky, so it would be safer to try to make a fire there than in the forest where she had spent the night. She went to work gathering small twigs and branches. She used some branches and long blades of grass to elevate the bamboo stalk. Then, under the bamboo, she gathered twigs and dry leaves. She used one of the matches from her grandmother to start a fire. She then filled the bamboo stalk with water from the river.

"Let's hope this works," Lihua said to Panpan. After a few minutes, the water in the bamboo stalk started to boil. "Yes!" Lihua said, jumping up and down. She was so excited she even added some of the huajiao peppercorns to the water. She found the leftover meat and vegetables from the night before, still by the river's edge. She washed them off and placed them into the boiling water as well.

"Look, Panpan," Lihua said. "I made hotpot!"

Panpan cocked her head curiously, and Lihua laughed.

When the bamboo was done cooking, Lihua used two twigs as chopsticks and dug into her little feast. It was one of the most delicious things she had ever eaten. Lihua ate her fill, and for the first time in days, she did not feel the gnawing pain of hunger in her stomach.

In fact, she felt strong, rested, and excited.

"I can do this," Lihua said to Panpan as she draped her bag over her shoulder. "*We* can do this. I won't starve. I won't freeze to death. No one will attack or kill me. As long as I have you, I can do this!"

Panpan ran up to Lihua and nuzzled her hand. Lihua petted her head and scratched her ears.

"Thank you, Panpan, for not giving up on me," Lihua said. "Are you ready? Let's go to the mountains!"

CHAPTER NINE

For the most part, Lihua and Panpan stayed by the river, only venturing back toward the road occasionally to make sure they were still walking in...well, if not the *right* direction at least *a* direction. Lihua no longer had any meat or vegetables or baozi, but the cooked bamboo with huajiao was enough to sustain her for now. Every evening, Panpan would make a small nest in the woods and Lihua would cook bamboo over a small fire by the river. Their little routine was quiet and a bit lonely, but it was safe. And, more importantly, it was working. Lihua was full, rested, and felt a bit more hopeful about the future. Of course, she had no plans beyond reaching the Dayong Mountains, but taking life one day at a time was enough for her right now.

She was chewing on some bamboo twigs as they walked when she was surprised to come across a temple in the middle of the forest. It wasn't even on the road. There was a small trail leading away from it that probably went back to the road, but she doubted many people would know it was here.

Lihua thought about her grandmother's admonition to stop and pray at every temple along her journey. She knew she should, but she was worried about Panpan. Panpan seemed unconcerned as she rolled around on the ground, scratching her back. But Lihua knew that as soon as she started walking toward the temple, Panpan would follow. The last thing she wanted was for Panpan to scare a monk to death.

They sat in the woods watching the temple for a long while, waiting to see if any petitioners would stop by or if any monks would come out. She was beginning to think the temple was abandoned when an old woman finally emerged. Her head was shaved and she was slightly hunched over. She also held a long stick out in front of her that she swung back and forth. Lihua realized the old nun was blind!

A younger nun then emerged from the temple holding a basket. She patted the old woman on the shoulder and then headed down the trail. Lihua thought the younger woman must have been going to a nearby town for supplies. If only the older blind nun were left, Lihua could easily sneak into the temple and say a prayer. Even if Panpan followed her, the nun wouldn't see her.

Lihua waited longer than necessary, both to build her courage and reassure herself that the younger nun was far away, before approaching the temple. As she suspected she would, Panpan followed.

"Be quiet, Panpan," Lihua said, her finger to her lips. "We can't let the nun know you are here."

The nun had gone back into the temple, but she reemerged as Lihua approached.

"Hello?" she called out. "Meiyin? Are you back already?"

"No," Lihua said. "I am just a traveler passing by and wanted to say a prayer."

The nun frowned. "You sound quite young. Are you traveling alone?"

Lihua paused before answering. She didn't want to lie to a nun, but she didn't want to alarm her either.

"I don't have any family," she answered truthfully. "I was on my way to Dayong and came across the temple."

The nun nodded. "Of course, child," she said, waving Lihua inside. "All are welcome here. But as you can see, we don't get many petitioners."

Lihua walked up the stone steps, Panpan following behind her. The nun turned her head, as though looking around for someone else. Lihua had a feeling that the nun's other senses were telling her they weren't alone, but since she couldn't see, she had no way of knowing for sure.

As they stepped through the door, the nun placed her arms around Lihua's shoulders, causing her to gasp. She hadn't been touched by another human in so long, she was surprised by the gentle wave of longing that rushed through her.

"You have been alone for some time, I think," the nun said.

Lihua shrugged. "I'm not sure. I think I left home only a few days ago...But it was never really my home." She raised her eyes up and was happy to see that the temple was dedicated to Guanyin. A large carving of the goddess looked down with a serene face upon Lihua. She felt her heart swell and did her best not to cry. She looked around the room for a distraction and realized that the temple was quite well taken care of. Everything looked clean and new, and several large windows and doors let in plenty of light.

Most temples were dark and dusty and quickly fell into disrepair since the monks didn't take in much money.

"This temple is beautiful," Lihua said.

The nun nodded. "When my husband died, I was a wealthy widow with only daughters who all married out, so I didn't have anyone to leave my money to. I used it to build this temple and take care of it for the rest of my days so I could live in peace."

"And the younger nun?" Lihua asked.

The nun raised an eyebrow. "How long were you out there?"

Lihua felt her face go hot. "I...I was scared..."

The nun held her tighter and nodded. "Meiyin is a niece of mine. Her betrothed died before they were wed, so she was forced to become a ghost bride. A widow before she was even married."

Lihua nodded her head sadly. She knew of ghost brides. It was a common custom. Women who were forced into widowhood without ever being brides or having children of their own, they were often lower than even slaves in the houses of their in-laws.

"That was kind of you to take her in," Lihua said.

"It was the least I could do," the nun said. "And I needed help after my eyesight went."

Lihua looked back and was relieved to see that Panpan was simply sitting in the doorway, watching. She then realized that Meiyin could come back at any moment.

"I'm sorry," Lihua said, pulling out of the nun's embrace and reaching into her bag to pull out a joss stick. "I cannot linger long. I need to keep going. I only wanted to say a prayer and pay my respects to the ancestors before moving on."

"Of course," the nun said, motioning to some candles in front of the statue of Guanyin.

Lihua lit the joss stick and then placed it with several others in front of the statue. Then she kneeled down and kowtowed, asking the goddess for protection and guidance on her journey. Then she stood up and bowed to the nun.

"Thank you," she said before turning to leave.

"Wait," the nun said. "You said you are going to Dayong? Why? What is there for you?"

Lihua shook her head, but then remembered that the nun couldn't see her. "Maybe nothing. But it is the only place I have heard mention of. I have to hope I will find something there."

"It is quite far," the nun said. "Hundreds of li. And the journey is dangerous."

Lihua felt her heart sink. "I...I have nowhere else to go."

The nun sighed. "I fear this journey will not lead you where you hope it will. And yet, if your heart is telling you that this is the direction you should go, who am I to discourage you? I can sense that you have prayed over this many times."

"So many times," Lihua said. "My grandmother told me to pray at every temple, and that is what I have done."

"Then perhaps the goddess is guiding you," the nun said. "She may have sent you to me for a reason. The best way for you to get to the mountains will be to take a boat."

"A boat?" Lihua asked, slightly alarmed. "Where would I find a boat?"

"Keep following the stream nearby. It will turn into a mighty river," the nun said. "You will find many men with bamboo boats who can take you to Dayong."

"Oh," Lihua said, unable to hide the disappointment in her voice. "I have no money. I cannot afford to hire a boat."

"You have no money?" the nun asked in surprise. "How have you survived?"

"I have been boiling bamboo shoots in the forest," Lihua said. "It's all I have eaten for days."

"Oh, my child," the nun said, embracing her. "There is such strength in you! If anyone can survive the journey that lies ahead, it is surely you. Wait here."

The nun walked over to the side of the room and through a door. When she emerged a moment later, she had a small bag with her filled with fruits and vegetables. She handed the bag to Lihua.

"No," Lihua said. "I cannot take food from a nun. I should be giving you all that I have." She reached into her bag and pulled out her small cloth of peppercorns, but the nun pushed her hand away and forced her to take the bag of food.

"I insist," she said. "And take this." She reached into her bag and pulled out a small coin purse, which she also gave to Lihua. "This is enough to hire a boat."

"I can't..." Lihua tried again, moved to tears by the kindness of the nun.

"You must," the nun said, closing Lihua's hands around the coin purse. "The goddess led you to me, and she also led me to help you. I only wish I could do more."

"You have done...so much," Lihua said, her eyes watering. "More than my own parents...or the people I thought were my parents..."

Panpan grunted and stood up, shifting from one foot to another anxiously. Lihua thought someone must be coming.

"What is that?" the nun asked. "Who is there? A dog?"

"No...not a dog," Lihua said as she stood and headed for the door. "But I must go. Thank you so much."

Panpan bounded down the steps and across the temple yard toward the forest. Lihua stepped through the door just as the nun grabbed her wrist. She turned back to face the woman.

"I will pray for you, my child," she said. "You will face more heartache before you find your way home, I think. But you must not give up. All life is suffering, but the goddess will not let you suffer forever."

Lihua wasn't sure how much comfort to take in the old nun's words, but she couldn't linger. She squeezed the woman's hand, thanked her again, and then ran down the steps and into the woods just as the young nun emerged down the path.

"What the...?" she heard the nun gasp. "Auntie! Auntie! A panda! Are you all right?"

"A panda..." Lihua heard the old nun gasp in disbelief. She felt bad for deceiving her, but what else could she have done? She only hoped the nun didn't rescind her offer to say a prayer on her behalf and put a curse on her instead.

Even after they got back to the creek, Lihua and Panpan kept running. It wasn't long before the creek widened into a river, just as the nun said it would.

There were many people along the river's edge fishing, selling goods, and manning bamboo boats. Lihua and Panpan sat in the woods watching the people as Lihua pondered what to do.

"We have to get on a boat, Panpan," Lihua said, "if we want to have a chance of making it to the mountains."

But she had no idea how to do that. To even approach any of the boatmen, she'd have to venture down to the river and talk to them, but she knew Panpan would follow her, causing a ruckus. Even if she managed to wave one of the men over and talk to them about taking her downriver, as soon as they saw Panpan, they would run away screaming. They would never agree to take a giant panda on one of their boats and row all the way to Dayong.

"Maybe we should wait until nightfall," Lihua said. "Then, I could talk to one of the boatmen without him seeing you, and then—"

Panpan let out a growl and burst out of the woods, running straight for the river.

"Panpan!" Lihua cried, running after her. "No!"

The people at the river looked up and saw the panda heading straight for them. A chorus of screams rang out as people started running in every direction. Some tried to grab their wares while others simply left everything behind in their haste to escape.

One man launched his boat into the river, thinking he could get away on the water, but Panpan headed for his boat instead of any of the others. As Panpan jumped on the boat, shoving it deeper into the water at the same time, the man screamed, leaping off the other end and swimming away.

Lihua got to the river's edge and ran into the water to the boat. She easily pulled herself up onto it and tossed her now soaked bag on the large bamboo stalks. The bamboo floated easily, naturally turning along with the current and drifting downstream.

"I'm sorry!" Lihua called out to the stunned boatman. She reached into her bag and pulled out the coin purse, tossing it to him as he swam back to shore. He caught it and then stared at her, dumbfounded.

Lihua used a paddle that was onboard to steer them into the middle of the river. The boat picked up speed.

"That was very naughty, Panpan," Lihua scolded. "But thanks anyway."

Panpan shook her whole body like a dog to dry off. Lihua turned her face to the sun as the wind blew through her hair.

She was sure they would be in the Dayong Mountains in no time.

CHAPTER TEN

The boat had a long oar attached to the back for steering and two smaller oars for paddling. Thankfully, Lihua didn't need to do much paddling. The river was wide and moved swiftly, so Lihua and Panpan were able to simply float along, enjoying the scenery.

Lihua was grateful for the food the nun had given her since there wasn't anything on the boat that she could eat. There had been a basket of fresh fish on board; the boatman must have just finished fishing when Panpan stole the boat. Lihua would have been happy to eat the fish if she had a way to cook it, but she didn't want to land on the shore unless it was absolutely necessary. She gave the fish to Panpan, who had no qualms about eating the fish raw, and she made due with the fruits and vegetables from the nun.

Lihua and Panpan passed many people while they floated down the river. Fishermen, other travelers, women on the banks washing clothes and collecting water to take back to their homes. Everyone watched Lihua and Panpan with wide-eyed fascination. Lihua waved to them all at first, proud of her panda companion. But eventually she got tired of the stares and tried to focus on the river ahead.

On the river, there was no protection from the sun, which beat down on them relentlessly. Lihua could feel her skin roasting and her insides baking. She continually used her water cup to collect fresh river water to pour over herself and Panpan, who lounged on the boat with two paws in the water for most of the day. They both longed for the night, when the sun set, the stars shined, and the peace and quiet of the river lulled them to sleep.

"What are you doing, little one?"

The voice of an older man startled Lihua awake one early morning. She picked up her oar and held it out in front of her. Panpan grunted and stood in a defensive pose. But the man, who was still on his own boat floating along next to her, only laughed.

The man was older, his skin dark and leathery from years spent on the river in the sun. He wore a woven conical hat, and he had several cormorant birds tied to his boat. She had seen many men using the cormorants to help them fish. The men tied a rope around the birds' throats to keep them from swallowing, so when the birds swooped into the water to grab the fish, they couldn't eat them, and the men could open the birds' beaks and pull out the fish.

"Believe me," the man said, "no one is going to attack a fairy with a panda god as her guardian."

"I'm not a fairy," Lihua said, lowering her guard as the man paddled his boat alongside hers.

"Who am I to say?" the man asked. "I've seen many strange things in my years on the river. Though, can't say I've ever seen a panda riding on a boat before."

"I was told the best way to get to the Dayong Mountains was by boat," Lihua said.

"You are going all the way to Dayong?" the man asked. "The river becomes very treacherous the closer you get to the mountains."

"Should we walk instead?" Lihua asked.

The man shook his head. "That might be more dangerous."

"What should I do?" Lihua asked.

"When you see a large rock in the river with the words 'come to me' carved on it, you should steer your boat straight for it," the man said.

Lihua tightened her grip on her oar. She didn't know much about steering a boat down a river, but that didn't sound right to her.

"Are you sure?" she asked.

"I haven't been there myself," the man said. "But I wouldn't want to anger your panda spirit by lying to you. Many experienced river men have told me this."

Panpan was distracted by one of the cormorants, swiping at it with her paw as it jumped from one boat to another.

Lihua had not considered that Panpan might not really be a panda, but a fairy or spirit in disguise. After all, Panpan had protected her many times. Maybe this was just one more way this panda fairy was keeping her safe.

"Thank you," Lihua finally said.

"Good luck, little one," the man said as he turned his boat away and steered back upstream.

"What do you think, Panpan?" Lihua asked. "Do you think we should steer straight into the rock?" She couldn't shake the lingering doubts telling her that such action was too dangerous. Maybe telling people to sail into the rock was the locals' way of sacrificing unsuspecting travelers to the river gods.

Panpan sighed as she went back to her place on the edge of the boat and dipped her paws into the cool water.

Late the next day, Lihua noticed that the river was picking up speed. Panpan moved to the center of the boat as the wind whipped over her fur. The boat bobbed up and down as the river started to churn.

"I think we might be getting close to the mountains, Panpan," Lihua said as she moved to the back of the boat and gripped onto the steering oar. She tried to keep them in the middle of the river, but for the most part, she could only go along with the current. She didn't have enough strength to steer the boat very well in such a strong flow.

Lihua and Panpan both shrieked as the boat plunged over a small fall in the river, leaving them drenched. Lihua crouched down next to Panpan to keep from being swept away.

The boat dipped to the left and right as the water rushed around an ever-increasing number of rocks jutting out of the river. Then, up ahead, Lihua could see the mountains. They were green and so tall they seemed to get lost in the clouds.

But she could not enjoy the view as the boat completely spun around in the turbulent river. She jumped back up and grabbed the steering oar. She had to make sure they at least kept going forward and didn't tip over.

Drenched and her teeth chattering, Lihua strained to see what was ahead of them.

"Panpan!" Lihua said, pointing. "There it is!"

Just as the man had said, there was a large rock with the characters "come to me" carved in it and painted red.

Lihua looked around, trying to see if there was another way to go. The river was still wide, and she thought it was possible that she could steer the boat far enough away from the rock to avoid it. She put all her weight into the steering oar, trying to force the boat away from the rock.

Panpan grunted at Lihua.

"If we crash into the rock, we will die!" Lihua said.

Panpan growled and nudged Lihua away from the steering oar. As soon as she let go, the boat lurched toward the stone. Lihua crouched down next to Panpan, hiding her head under her arms.

"I sure hope you are right about this!" Lihua cried. "Please, protect us!" she cried out to any god or ancestor who might have been listening.

As the boat headed straight for Come to Me Rock, Lihua screamed. The boat dipped, rocked, and jutted to the left, just skirting around the rock at the last moment. Then, the river stilled.

"We did it!" Lihua said, hugging Panpan. Then, she stood up.

She was surrounded by the Dayong Mountains.

On both sides of the river, the mountains stood so high she could not see the tops of them, and they were blanketed in every color of green. The air was so fresh and clean, it was as though she had never really breathed before.

White clouds slowly encircled the mountains and then settled over the river. It started to drizzle. And then it started to rain.

Lihua sighed in annoyance. What sort of welcome was this after such a long journey?

She saw a sandy bank along the river's edge to dock the boat at and steered toward it. They were still traveling swiftly as they landed, so the boat slipped all the way up onto the shore. Lihua and Panpan ran to the ground, so happy to feel dirt and rocks beneath their feet again.

"Now what?" Lihua asked Panpan.

Panpan shook her body to rid herself of the rainwater, but it didn't help. She then wandered into the woods. Lihua followed Panpan as she did what she always did—make a small nest in the grass.

Lihua lifted her head as the rain fell on her face.

"I can't sleep in the rain like you, Panpan," Lihua said. She headed back to the boat, and Panpan followed.

Lihua lifted the bamboo boat up to try and drag it into the woods, but she wasn't strong enough. The boat was surprisingly heavy for something that floated so well.

Panpan slipped under the boat and helped Lihua carry it into the woods. Once they were at Panpan's nest, Lihua lifted the boat higher and propped it up on a tree, covering the nest and protecting it from the rain.

Lihua and Panpan then climbed into the nest and collapsed from exhaustion. Even though they were both soaking wet, the air was warm, and it was nice not having the rain continue to pelt them.

"Welcome to Dayong, Panpan," Lihua said.

Panpan huffed as she curled into a ball.

Lihua laid next to the panda, but she couldn't sleep. Not at first. She was here. She made it. Despite everything, she reached her goal. She had survived and done what should have been impossible.

For the first time since she left her home, she felt hopeful. Maybe it was foolish. After all, she was in the middle of nowhere with no food and no family. Was she just going to live here in the mountains with her panda for the rest of her life? Maybe. She could cook bamboo and now had some fishing equipment. Once it stopped raining, she could build a fire and make a small feast for herself.

She smiled to herself. She was tired and hungry and wet now, but tomorrow was a new day. And she had a plan. First, she would eat. Then, she would figure out a more permanent shelter.

She could do this, she told herself as she drifted off.

She could do this.

CHAPTER ELEVEN

By morning, the rain had stopped. Sunlight filtered in through the trees, warming Lihua as she snuggled by Panpan's side. The birds were singing and she could hear monkeys hooting in the distance. She felt at peace here. She felt safe. The only thing encouraging her from leaving the little den she and Panpan had built was the hunger rumbling in her stomach.

"Come on, Panpan," she said as she sat up and stretched her arms.

Panpan yawned, her mouth wide, revealing her many long, sharp teeth.

Lihua smiled to herself at the knowledge that she had no reason to fear this big, strong mama bear. Panpan was her only friend—her only family—in the whole world, and she was grateful to have her. After only a couple of weeks together, they were inseparable. Even though Lihua knew that one day she would have to find more humans, she hoped that she could find a way to keep Panpan in her life. Maybe she could marry a farmer and they could live near the woods. They could build a small barn that Panpan could sleep in.

They crawled out from under the raft and walked back down to the river. Lihua breathed in the crisp air, but then she gasped as something pungent invaded her nose.

"Ugh, what is that smell?" she asked.

Panpan ambled up to her side and grunted.

Lihua sniffed her shirt. "Eww. It's me!" She looked up and down the river and listened for a long time. She didn't hear any sounds of human life. They were completely alone in this place. Lihua took off her bag and realized it was still soaked. She took everything out of it, including her joss sticks and matches, and laid them on the rocks so they could dry. She then took off her own clothes and did her best to wash them in the river with the soap she had taken from the women early in their journey before laying them out to dry as well. Then she jumped into the river and washed.

"Come on, Panpan!" Lihua called. "The water's great!" But Panpan only grunted and wrinkled her nose.

Since it was summer, the river water was a perfect temperature. Not too hot, not too cold. Lihua reached down to the bottom of the river and pulled up handfuls of silty mud. She rubbed it over her body and then rinsed it off. She floated on her back, letting her hair drift around her. She imagined she sprouted fins and could swim all the way to the ocean. But then she remembered the cormorant fishermen and decided that was too dangerous. Besides, what did she need fins for? She had two perfectly good legs. She could walk anywhere she wanted to go. She was completely free to do whatever she wanted.

And yet, she missed her parents. In spite of everything, if she thought of them, she felt a sharp pain in her chest.

She still didn't really understand what had happened. She knew she wasn't related to them, not really, but she loved them. Wasn't it possible they could have loved her in return? She was certain her grandmother had loved her. Her grandmother never would have sent her away if she had the money to keep her.

She thought about her baby brother. She had prayed for him to come, prayed for Mama to have a safe pregnancy and birth. And when Lihua saw him for the first time, her heart swelled to bursting. They weren't related, but she loved him from before he was born. No matter what happened, she would always remember her little brother. She would carry him in her heart for the rest of her days.

She vowed that if she ever had a chance to love a child, whether it was hers or not, she would never abandon it.

She shook her head to clear away the gloomy thoughts. The past was over. She could never go back home. Even if she wanted to, she would never find it again. She didn't even know the name of her village—she had never needed to know it. She swam back to the shore and put her clothes back on. They were still wet, but she didn't have a way to dry them or herself. Hopefully she would dry in the bright mountain sun. Her other items were still a bit damp, so she left them to continue drying while she and Panpan went into the woods to find some bamboo she could cook.

When she got back, the matches were dry enough to start a fire, which she used to cook the bamboo and finish drying her clothes. As she sat by the river, letting her food settle, she wished it were possible to simply live here. But she would need a sturdier shelter. Her clothes were wearing out, and she needed more to eat than just bamboo. She finally sighed and accepted the fact that even though she had reached her destination, they needed to keep moving. She couldn't stay here forever—or even for very long.

She collected her few belongings and put them back into her bag. As she did so, something glinted in the bottom of the bag. She reached in and pulled out the silver baby bracelet her grandmother said she had been wearing when her parents bought her. She supposed that, if nothing else, she could eventually sell it and buy some food. She put the bracelet in her pocket and put everything else back into her bag. She plaited her hair and tied the ends together with a reed from the water's edge. Then she and Panpan headed away from the river and into the forest.

As they walked, they slowly made their way up the side of one of the mountains. The higher they climbed, the more breathtaking the view became. She seemed to be surrounded by hundreds of spires jutting up into the sky. She couldn't even see the tops of many of them, they were so tall. But when she climbed one of the spires high enough, she couldn't see the ground anymore! The trees were so thick below her, it was as though she were floating in the sky.

"I think this place must be full of old magic," Lihua said.

Panpan let out a sigh as she munched on some wild berries that Lihua didn't eat for fear they could be poisonous.

"If you're some kind of fairy, Panpan," Lihua said, "I think you should reveal yourself to me. We are safe here. You can be honest with me."

Panpan walked up to Lihua and licked her face, then she continued walking up the mountain.

Lihua wiped the slobber away and sighed. "Fine," she said. "Maybe you are a real panda and not a fairy. But there is something special about you, I'm sure of it."

As they walked along, Lihua stopped when the bushes next to her shook.

"Who's there?" she asked, but there was no response, only more rustling.

Panpan walked over and sniffed at the brush. Then she stepped forward, pushing further into the leaves.

Lihua gasped when a small monkey jumped out and grabbed onto a nearby branch. The monkey chittered at Panpan in annoyance.

"How cute!" Lihua exclaimed, holding her hand out. "Come here, little one. I won't hurt you."

The small brown monkey with a red face cocked its head at her and made more chittering sounds.

Panpan stepped back and huffed.

Lihua took a step forward, still with her arm outstretched. She really wanted to pet the monkey.

"Come on, baby," she cooed, even though she had no way of knowing how old the monkey was.

Then, a larger monkey dropped down next to the smaller one and stood in a protective stance, baring its teeth.

Lihua stepped back slowly. "Sorry," she said. "I didn't mean to scare you."

The larger monkey let out some hoots, which were answered by several others.

Lihua looked up and her eyes went wide when she saw that there were dozens of monkeys in the trees surrounding them.

"Hello, everyone," she said softly, and some of the monkeys crept down from the trees toward her.

The larger monkey close to her jumped down from its protective place over the smaller monkey to the ground and walked up to Lihua. The monkey walked around her, picking at her clothes and her bag.

"I'm sorry, I don't have anything for you," Lihua said.

The monkey then jumped up onto her back and tugged at her hair.

Panpan grunted and stepped forward.

"It's okay...I think," Lihua said. "She's just curious. Right, monkey?"

The monkey tugged at Lihua's ears and poked her nose. Some of the other monkeys jumped down and came close as well.

Lihua started to feel a bit nervous as the monkey on her back examined her face. She could see that the monkey had fangs and could probably bite rather hard if she wanted to. She had also heard that monkeys were dirty creatures that carried illnesses. She did not want to get some kind of monkey sickness.

Lihua slowly raised a hand for the monkey to sniff, then she gently petted one of the monkey's arms. The monkey looked at her hand curiously, but did not react. Lihua then pressed her hand against the monkey's shoulder to urge her to jump away.

The monkey seemed to take offense at this and began to hoot and holler, but it did jump away onto a nearby tree. This caused the other monkeys to start jumping and hollering as well.

"Okay, okay!" Lihua tried to say, but she wasn't sure they could hear her. "I'm sorry!"

Panpan had finally had enough. She let out a growl and stepped aggressively toward the monkeys that had surrounded Lihua. This made the monkeys shriek louder. Several of them began to climb on Lihua, pulling at her hair and clothes.

Lihua was now scared. She knew that it was only a matter of time before one of the monkeys bit her. She pulled her arms up to her face, and the quick movement caused several of the monkeys to scatter away from her. She used the opportunity to back away from the group of monkeys, but she felt something tugging at her shirt. She looked down and saw that one of the monkeys had taken her baby bracelet from her pocket.

Lihua didn't think before yelling, "Hey! Give that back!"

The monkey screeched at her, bearing its fangs to her, but Lihua only felt angry.

"That is mine!" she said, stepping forward. "Give it to me."

The monkey turned and ran away under the brush.

"Panpan!" Lihua said as she tried to follow the monkey. "Don't let it get away."

Panpan let out a fearsome growl and crashed through the undergrowth after the monkey.

The monkey and Panpan were both much faster than Lihua, but she followed as quickly as she could. The other monkeys followed, swinging from tree to tree above them, screeching and hollering the whole way.

Lihua watched in horror as one of the monkeys dropped from the tree onto Panpan's back and scratched at her. Panpan growled and spun around quickly, trying to knock the monkey loose. Lihua grabbed a branch off the ground and swung it at the monkey, scaring it away. Panpan then went after the thieving monkey again.

The monkey climbed up on a log and leaped away, but Panpan grabbed it by the tail with her mouth, dragging it back down.

"You did it!" Lihua exclaimed, but her excitement turned to horror as she watched Panpan stumble over the log. Panpan grunted and the monkey screeched as they both fell. The monkeys in the trees over them all hooted in terror as well.

Lihua ran to the log and looked over the other side. The log had obscured the edge of a ravine. Panpan and the monkey were both now at the bottom, not moving.

"Panpan?" Lihua called, but the panda didn't move. "Panpan!" Lihua screamed.

CHAPTER TWELVE

"Panpan! No! Panpan!" Lihua called out over and over again as she paced at the top of the ravine. This couldn't be happening. She couldn't lose Panpan. She couldn't be alone, not again. Not now. Not here in this unfamiliar place.

The monkeys overhead continued to jump and screech, but neither Panpan nor the monkey in the ravine moved.

"Shut up!" Lihua finally yelled at the monkeys, waving her arms at them to go away. "Get out of here, you filthy beasts! This is all your fault!"

The monkeys screeched back at her, but one by one, they started to leave. Lihua looked back below and saw that the monkey was partially under Panpan. It must have been crushed. There was no way it could have survived. She had a feeling the other monkeys knew their friend was dead, so that was why they were leaving.

But Panpan was bigger and stronger than a monkey. Even though she wasn't moving, she might have survived. She was probably just unconscious. Maybe she hit her head on the way down. Lihua would just have to wait until Panpan woke up. She wouldn't abandon her friend.

She looked around for a safe way down, but she didn't see one. The sides of the ravine were steep and looked wet from the rain. They were also covered in a bright green moss. If she tried to climb down, she would surely slip and fall, then they would both be trapped.

Which brought her to the next problem. If—no, *when* Panpan woke up, how would she get out of the ravine? Lihua didn't see an obvious path up. But animals could often go where humans couldn't. Panpan had claws. While it would probably be impossible for Lihua to climb out, Panpan might have no trouble. Lihua would just have to wait and see what happened. First, Panpan needed to wake up. Lihua had to have faith that she would wake up. She didn't want to think about what she would have to do if Panpan died.

Lihua sat down and did her best not to cry. She cursed to herself. She might have lost her panda over that stupid bracelet. Why did she care about it so much? She didn't even know it existed only a few days ago. And what did it mean anyway? It was given to her by her birth parents who either lost her or sold her. They obviously didn't care about her. If her adoptive parents who raised her didn't care about her, how could people who only knew her for a few months back when she was just a baby?

She felt the tears prick her eyes and she lowered her face to her knees. Her heart hurt. She tried to tell herself that her birth parents must not, could not have loved her, but then she thought about Panpan. She had only known Panpan—who wasn't even a human—for a short while, but she already felt she couldn't live without her. And then she remembered Panpan's baby. Even though the baby had died, Panpan didn't want to leave it. She had slept with the baby in her nest until Lihua buried it. If Lihua had not come along, Panpan would probably still be by the baby's side.

She then remembered her little brother. She had only known him for the briefest of moments. She had touched his hair. Breathed in his scent. She had never even held him, yet she knew that she would do anything to protect him. She had lost everything for him. She left her home so he could have the best future possible. If the family could only have one child, she let it be him.

And she didn't even know his name.

She had been angry and hurt and would have told herself anything to keep from thinking about how much her birth parents might have loved her. She wasn't sure which hurt more—the idea that her birth parents didn't love her and willfully gave her away, or the idea that they did love her and were sick over the loss of her. Did it matter if they did love her? She could never find them. Would never see them again. If she let herself think that they loved her, she would have to mourn the loss of them as well. She didn't think she could bear the loss of two families at once—one of which she had never even known.

But what else could she do?

She cried silently. She lifted her head and looked up as the sunlight dimmed through the trees. Day would soon turn to night. She didn't want to think about facing the nighttime forest alone without Panpan to protect her and keep her warm.

She sat up and looked back into the ravine again. "Panpan?" she called out softly, her hope waning.

To her surprise, she heard a low growl.

"Panpan!" she cried.

Down below, Panpan stirred.

"You're alive! Thank the gods!" Lihua said.

Panpan grunted as she raised her head, giving it a shake. Then she slowly stood and stretched her legs. The monkey below her still did not move. It was surely dead.

Lihua reached down into the pit. "Come on, girl," she said. "You need to get out of there."

Panpan raised her head and looked around. She reared up on her hind legs and pawed at the side of the ravine, but she couldn't get a solid grip. As Lihua had feared, Panpan was trapped.

She looked around to try and figure out what to do. If she had been trapped down there, how would she get out? She would need a way to climb up. Maybe a rope. No, that wouldn't work for a panda. She was too heavy and couldn't grip a rope with her claws.

Maybe some kind of ladder? But what could she use to make a ladder? Bamboo! The men in her village often used bamboo ladders when they needed to do work high up on buildings or in trees. It would take a lot of work to make a ladder, though. She would need two long, sturdy bamboo poles, and then several smaller ones to make the rungs. Then how would she secure the rungs to the poles? And could she make the rungs strong enough for a panda?

Panpan let out a frustrated roar.

"I know!" Lihua replied, exasperated. "I'm trying to think of something." She rubbed her head and paced. Building a ladder was probably too hard and wouldn't work for a panda. There had to be another way. She looked back down at Panpan, her sharp claws gripping on the slick rocky wall of the ravine, and she realized that pandas were very good climbers. Panpan might not be able to climb straight up, but if she only had a slight incline, something she could grip onto, she could probably make her way out.

"I got it!" Lihua said. She might not be able to make a ladder, but bamboo was still the answer. If she just had enough bamboo logs, Panpan could use them to climb out. She didn't see any here she could use. The solid trees were too strong for her to pull down on her own. And any laying around on the ground were too fragile to support a panda's weight. But she knew where she could find several strong bamboo logs already cut.

"Just wait here, Panpan. I have an idea." It would be hard, but she knew how to get Panpan out of the ravine.

She ran down the mountain and back toward the river, to the nest she and Panpan had made the night before with the bamboo raft. She pulled out her knife and cut the ropes that were tying the bamboo stalks together. One by one, she dragged the bamboo logs up the mountain to the ravine. She didn't put them in the ravine yet. She was worried that Panpan might try to climb them before there were enough and would snap them under her weight. As she dragged the bamboo logs up the mountain, she thought her heart would burst from the exertion and her legs felt like jelly.

"Come on..." she grunted to herself as she forced one leg in front of another. "You can do it..."

Finally, she had three logs at the top of the ravine. She prayed that together they would be strong enough to support Panpan's weight. She put the bamboo logs into the ravine at an angle. She hadn't considered if they were tall enough to reach from the bottom to the top, but thankfully, they were.

"Hurry, Panpan!" she called as soon as all three logs were lined up together in the ravine. Then she held her breath.

Panpan cautiously stepped onto the bamboo, bouncing up and down to make sure they would hold her weight. Once she was convinced it was safe, she quickly scuttled up the logs and out of the ravine!

"You did it!" Lihua yelled as she ran to Panpan and nearly collapsed as she wrapped her arms around her friend. For some reason, she then burst into tears. She didn't understand it. She thought that she would be excited when Panpan climbed out. She felt so proud of herself for figuring out how to rescue Panpan on her own. And yet, all she felt was utter despair. The thought of losing her friend was too much for her. She was scared and exhausted.

"Come on," Lihua said. She may have lost the bracelet, but at least she still had Panpan. Together, they climbed back down the mountain to the nest. Even though it was no longer covered, they didn't have anywhere else to go. It was the closest thing to a bed they had.

Once they arrived back at the nest, Lihua and Panpan both curled up and quickly fell asleep.

CHAPTER THIRTEEN

Even though she was hungry the next morning when she awoke, Lihua had no desire to climb out of the nest. Her whole body was sore from dragging the bamboo up the mountain, and she couldn't stop thinking about her parents—her birth ones and adoptive ones. If she slept, she wouldn't have to wonder about them and feel a hurt in her heart.

The mountains had lost their appeal as well. She didn't know what she expected. It was foolish to come here, where she knew no one and nothing. The forest was too dangerous. She'd almost been killed by a pack of wild monkeys. What would she do if she came across a truly dangerous animal, like a tiger? Or what if she had fallen into the ravine? She might never have found a way out.

She realized that if she tried to stay in the mountains alone, even with Panpan, she would die. She finally forced herself to sit up and leave the nest. She went back to the river and washed her face. She watched the water shimmer in the sunlight. Suddenly, she remembered the fishing equipment that had been on the boat. It had been raining when they pulled up on the shore, so where had it gone? She walked along the edge of the river, looking around rocks and bushes. She finally found the fishing pole, complete with a line and hook, but the basket for fish was gone. Panpan had eaten all the fish anyway. Lihua dug in the mud for some worms and baited the hook, then she threw the line into the river. To her surprise, she caught a fish almost immediately. And it was a fairly good size too.

"Look at this, Panpan!" she said, holding up her catch proudly.

Panpan sat up and waved her paws, like she was begging for a treat. Lihua tossed Panpan the fish, which she ate in two bites.

Lihua tossed out the line again and caught another fish. She should have known these would be good fishing waters. With no people around, the river must have been thick with fish. Panpan looked at Lihua with pleading eyes.

"Oh no," Lihua said as she laid her fish on a rock. "This one is for me." But before long, Lihua had more than enough fish for both of them. They walked back to where Lihua had made a fire the day before and made a new one. She realized that she would soon run out of matches if she weren't careful. Another reason to try and find people.

Lihua gutted the fish and stuffed some of the huajiao peppercorns inside, then she laid the fish over the fire to cook. Once the fish were done grilling, she ate them eagerly. She nearly moaned as she ate, the fish was so delicious. Not to mention how pleasurable it was to eat something besides bamboo.

She ate her fill of the fish and felt better. She reminded herself how important it was to eat. Not only to keep her from starving to death, but to help her mind stay clear and to give her energy for the day ahead.

"I suppose we should try to find people, Panpan," Lihua said. "We can't go back, and we don't have any reason to keep moving. If we find a village, I can ask if anyone needs a worker. I can cook and clean. Surely someone will need a kitchen helper. They wouldn't even have to pay me. If they just provide some food and a place to sleep, it would be more than I have now."

Panpan whimpered and cocked her head.

"You can live anywhere," Lihua said. "If you make a nest in the woods nearby, I'll come visit you every day. But...I just can't live like a bear. It's too dangerous."

Panpan huffed.

"If we find one village, we can find more," Lihua said. "If no one in the first village needs a worker, then we check at the next one, and the next."

Panpan moaned and shook her head.

"I don't have any other plans," Lihua said. "I...I don't have a place in this world. I come from nowhere and have nowhere to go. I just have to start over."

She looked up and down the river, across the water to the other side, and behind her at the mountain. "If we find any people to start over with, anyway," she mumbled. She shook her head. No point in wallowing. She wasn't going to find anyone sitting here. She packed up her few belongings in her bag and slung it over her shoulder. She fastened the fishing pole to the bag as well.

"Let's start walking," she said to Panpan.

Panpan grunted and then moved into a squatting position.

"Of course, you would wait until I'm ready to leave to poop," Lihua said, turning her back on Panpan to give her some privacy. After a few minutes, she heard Panpan whimpering. "What's wrong?"

Panpan shuffled back and forth on her feet near the pile of poo she had made.

"Yes, you pooped," Lihua said. "Can we go now?"

Panpan grunted and dug at the poop with her foot.

"Eww! Panpan! Stop!" Lihua said, stomping over. When she got close, Panpan looked intently at the poop.

Lihua wrinkled her nose as she looked at it too. Something glinted.

"Panpan," Lihua asked in amazement. "Is that...?" She reached into the poop and picked the item up.

It was her silver bracelet!

"You got it back!" Lihua exclaimed. She had thought the bracelet was gone forever. She hadn't even looked for it down in the pit. She wouldn't have risked getting trapped down there herself going after it. When Panpan grabbed the monkey with her jaw, she must have somehow swallowed the bracelet.

She walked over the river and rinsed the poo off the bracelet. As she washed it, it seemed to shine even more than it had before. She held it up to the light and looked closely at the markings.

"Is that..." She squinted. "Two...one...nine...These are numbers." Lihua couldn't read many characters, but she knew a few, especially numbers since she worked in her parents' noodle shop. "Do you think..." She felt something in her chest swelling, but she was afraid to hope. "Do you think this could be my birthday?"

Panpan walked over next to her as if to get a better look.

"There is more written here," Lihua observed, running her thumb over the characters. "I can't make them out. But if we find someone who can read, maybe they can tell me what it says."

Panpan grunted happily.

"Nainai said that the baby seller brought me from Changsha," Lihua said. "We now know where I'm from and the date I was born. I know it's not much, but it's something. If I was stolen instead of sold, my parents might be looking for me. If I go back, if I look for them too, maybe...maybe we will find each other."

She knew it was probably too much to hope for. She had no idea where Changsha was or how big the city could be. Children probably went missing every day there. Her parents might not want to find her. The odds were completely against her.

But the odds had always been against her. She should have been killed by those bad men on the road the first day. She should have starved by now. She should have drowned in the river. Obstacles had been put in her path every step of the way and she had managed to overcome them. Why should this be any different?

And as she had told Panpan earlier, she didn't have anywhere else to go. Why not have a goal of traveling to Changsha? It couldn't be any better or worse than any other place. At least it gave her something to work toward. A plan. A reason to keep going.

And yet, as she looked around, seeing no signs of human life, she had no idea which way to go. She had destroyed their boat, so they had no way to keep floating down the river in order to find a village.

Then she heard screaming from across the river.

Lihua looked and saw several women in red dresses waving at her and pointing. She was confused at first, but then she realized that they were trying to warn her that Panpan was right behind her. They thought that Panpan was a dangerous wild animal. She almost laughed when she realized what they were trying to tell her. Instead, she threw her arms around Panpan to show them that Panpan was friendly.

The women gasped, then they burst into laughter. They waved her over to them. She held her arms up, asking how she was supposed to cross, and they made swimming motions with their arms.

"I guess we are going to get wet again, Panpan," Lihua said with a sigh. Panpan groaned, but she followed as Lihua began to wade across the river. At its deepest point, the river only came up to Lihua's chest, so she held her bag over her head as she crossed to avoid getting her matches and joss sticks wet again.

As Lihua reached the other side of the river, the women laughed and fussed over her, helping her out and carrying her bag. Even though Lihua had shown them Panpan was friendly, the women still screamed and ran away as Panpan emerged from the river and shook her fur wildly to dry off.

"It's okay," Lihua said. "She's my friend."

The women began to speak excitedly, but she couldn't understand them. It took her a moment to realize they were speaking a completely different language.

"I'm sorry," Lihua tried to tell them. "I don't understand." She shrugged her shoulders and held up her hands helplessly to show she didn't know what they were saying.

The women finally nodded and moaned in disappointment when they realized she didn't speak their language.

"Are you a fairy?" one of the older girls finally asked Lihua in a language nearer to her own.

Lihua laughed. "What? Me? I'm no one."

"But the...the bear," the girl stammered as she tried to remember the word for panda. "You must be blessed by the gods to travel with such a companion."

"Maybe the bear is the fairy!" one of the other girls exclaimed, and they all burst into laughter.

Lihua shook her head. "No. You all are very kind, but I am just...I'm just an orphan who has no home. Panpan is a panda who lost her baby. We are just trying to find a new place to live."

The girls translated amongst each other and slowly nodded their heads in understanding. Finally, the oldest girl took Lihua's hand in her own.

"You will come with us," the girl said.

Lihua was so shocked by the warmth of the girl's touch, she nearly lost her bladder. She almost jerked her hand back instinctively.

The girl seemed to sense Lihua's hesitation. She gave Lihua a reassuring smile and slid her arm around her shoulder, leading her down a well-worn forest path. Lihua looked back and saw that Panpan was following, surrounded by the other girls who were so excited to touch a panda. They gathered up their unwashed laundry and empty water jugs. They must have come to the river to complete their chores, but were now too distracted.

Lihua and Panpan were taken to the girls' village, which was nestled along the side of a mountain in the trees. It looked nothing like her old village. Instead of the area being completely cleared of trees, the dark wood houses with black slate roofs seemed to be built among the forest, giving it a natural feel. The houses were sturdy and multi-storied. As she got closer, she realized the buildings didn't have a first floor at all, but were built on stilts! She wondered how the whole village didn't fall over.

As they walked through the village, everyone seemed to come out to see Lihua and Panpan. The children squealed with delight and the men held their hands to their mouths in shock. The people all wore colorful clothes, mostly in shades of red, like the women she met at the river.

An elderly man approached them. He was wearing a long blue tunic and his head was wrapped in white linen. The girls all gave him a respectful bow, so Lihua did as well. The older girl then spoke to the man in their own language. The man nodded.

"Welcome to our village," he said in a dialect Lihua could understand. "Welcome to you and your panda."

Lihua's eyes watered. She tried to give an appreciative nod, but she felt her legs give way beneath her. She collapsed and everything went black.

CHAPTER FOURTEEN

Lihua woke with a start. She was in a darkened room with a brazier burning in the middle. She was wearing dry clothes and was covered with a blanket. She felt her pants and sighed in relief to find that the silver bracelet was in her pocket. Whoever changed her clothes must have found it and put it where she was sure to find it.

The door was open, and Panpan was laying curled up just outside. When Panpan saw that Lihua was awake, she lumbered over and licked Lihua's face. Lihua squeezed her neck.

"Wh-where are we?" Lihua asked, her voice cracking.

The older girl she had met by the river rushed to her side with a cup of tea. "You're safe. You must have been very tired."

Lihua nodded and sipped at the tea. It was soothing and helped settle her nervous stomach. She couldn't remember when she had last slept so deeply or comfortably. The girl led her to the other side of the room where a bucket of warm water sat. The girl helped her wash her hair and her body and then gave her some clean clothes to wear. She then led Lihua back to the pallet of blankets she had been sleeping on.

"I'll get food," the girl said. As she left, the old man Lihua had seen just before she passed out entered the room.

"I am glad you are finally awake," he said as he sat on a small stool next to her. "We were worried about you."

"I am sorry," Lihua said. "I don't know what happened."

"I think you, and your panda," he said looking at Panpan, who was sitting nearby, "have traveled a long way."

"I think so," Lihua said, "but I don't really know. When I left my village, I walked and walked. Then we took a boat down the river."

The man nodded. "Your body and mind were exhausted. I think you collapsed because this was the first time in many days you felt safe. You needed the rest."

Lihua's eyes watered. "Who are you?"

"I am the village timo," the man said, his chest puffing up a bit. "A shaman."

"I don't know what that is," Lihua said sheepishly.

The timo hmphed. "People today, they forget the old ways."

"I pray," Lihua said. "My grandmother taught me. I have kneeled before every ancestor temple I have passed."

The old man smiled, his eyes twinkling. "I think they have heard you."

"Have they?" Lihua asked. "Then why have I suffered so?"

"All life is suffering," the man said. "But why else would they send you a panda spirit to guide you?"

Panpan grunted and wrinkled her nose.

Lihua leaned in and whispered to the timo conspiratorially. "I think she's a fairy in disguise."

The timo nodded his agreement. "The spirit world is not a place of rest. Those who reside there are often on their own journeys. This panda will not leave you until her own quest is complete."

Lihua pondered over these words. She had hoped that Panpan would never leave her. That they could find a way to stay together. But his words seemed to be telling her that, eventually, Panpan would have to move on. She tried not to feel sad at learning this. For now, they were together. And they would stick together for as long as possible.

At that, the girl, and a few others, came back with several plates of food. It was more food and more variety than she had ever seen at once in her life! Rice, corn, beans, dumplings, fried fish, pickled vegetables, and more. The older girl took a round rice cake, filled it with honey, and handed it to Lihua. She sighed as she ate it. She'd never had anything so delectable. The rest of the food was spicy and sour. It was not spicy the same way her huajiao was, but it was still delicious. The girls also brought Panpan a large stack of bamboo shoots, which Panpan was more than happy to munch on.

Lihua had only eaten a few bites of each dish when she started to feel an ache in her stomach. She was surprised because she felt like she had hardly eaten anything and only moments ago had been starving. She held her head in shame as she pushed the food away.

"I'm so sorry," she said. "But it is simply too much food. I couldn't eat another bite."

The old man and the girls looked at each other sadly.

"How long have you been on the road, little cub?" the timo asked.

Lihua could not stop the tears from falling. "I...I don't know. I have lost track of the time."

The man placed a gentle hand on her shoulder. "You have been through a terrible ordeal. Do not push yourself too hard. Stay here. Rest. Eat."

"I couldn't," Lihua said. "You have done too much for me already."

"I insist," the timo said. He stood and left the room. "I will return tomorrow." The other girls collected the food dishes and then left the room as well. Lihua laid down next to Panpan.

"What is happening?" she asked. "These people are being so kind to us. I don't understand it."

These strangers had shown her more kindness and generosity than her own parents had. She was both grateful and leery. But she was still too exhausted to make sense of it.

When Lihua woke the next day, she felt better than she had since she left her village. She stood and peeked through the door of her room. She watched as the villagers went about their morning business. She saw several people with farming equipment and baskets heading out to the rice and corn fields. Some children were tending their goats. And several women were weaving long colorful cloths. As she went down the stairs, Panpan followed her. The children ran over to see the panda and everyone else smiled at her.

The timo walked over from a house and greeted her. "How are you feeling today?" he asked.

"Much better," she said. Indeed, her upset stomach seemed to have subsided and she was hungry again.

"Come," he said, and he led her to what she thought must have been his own house. Panpan sat outside with the children who fed her bamboo shoots and stalks of sugar-cane. The timo's wife served Lihua a bowl of congee with fish. Lihua thought that since the village was near the river, many of their meals probably consisted of fish.

After they ate, the timo took her to a central room where there were many statues of gods and ancestor tablets. It was like a temple in their home.

"We set your clothes and other things out to dry and found your matches and joss sticks," he said. "And you mentioned that you prayed at temples along your journey. Even though these are not your ancestors, I thought you might want to pray to them."

Lihua thanked him and kneeled before the carvings. He handed her not one, but several joss sticks and helped her light them and place them in the offering tray. He then raised his eyes and his hands and recited several prayers and blessings in his own language. Lihua didn't understand him, but she kowtowed to the ancestors anyway.

"I told the ancestors to look out for you as one of our own," the timo said as he stood.

"Thank you," Lihua said as she followed him back outside. They went back to the village center and sat on a bench where they could watch Panpan and the children play. "I don't know why you and your people have been so kind to me. I am no one."

"No one?" the timo asked with surprise. "You have blessed us with the panda spirit. You have given us more than we can ever repay."

Lihua couldn't tell if the timo was joking or not. It

sounded preposterous, but it wasn't every day a panda entered a village and played with the children.

"Where are you going?" the timo asked.

"To Changsha, I think," Lihua said, pulling out her bracelet and handing it to him. "I was sold by a man who said he was from Changsha. I think that is where I might find my birth parents."

The timo took the bracelet and looked at it closely. "These markings look like a date," he said, pointing to the numbers. "Probably your birth date. These characters here say 'Kaifu.' Kaifu is a district of Changsha."

Lihua's heart fluttered. She now knew what part of Changsha to look in. She was even closer to finding her parents!

"These other characters," the timo said, "I don't recognize. I think they might be the mark of the silversmith."

Lihua took the bracelet back and looked closer at the markings. "If I find the man who made this, do you think he will know who my parents are?"

The timo chuckled. "I'm sure he makes many bracelets for many parents. But it will be as good a start as any. If you are sure you still want to go."

"What do you mean?" Lihua asked. "Of course, I want to go. I'm so close!"

"Changsha is still quite far," the timo said. "It would take you weeks to get there by foot."

Lihua felt her heart drop. "Oh."

"Not to mention that this area is very dangerous," he went on. "The warlords, the communists, the Kuomintang, everyone is fighting. There are bandits, poachers, traffickers, opium runners. You have come a long way, but I would not feel safe letting a little cub such as you go back out on the road."

"What do you mean?" Lihua asked.

"You could stay here," he said. "We could find you plenty of work to do and give you a place to sleep and food to eat in exchange. And when you are old enough, we could find you a husband."

Lihua's heart beat fast. It was what she had originally wanted. To find a place where she would be safe and cared for. And the people here already knew about Panpan and accepted her as well. They thought she was a blessing! This could be the answer to her prayers!

But then she squeezed the bracelet in her hand. She looked around at the children with their parents. She looked at how the people all dressed the same and the strange food they ate. These were good people. Kind people. But this wasn't her home.

"Thank you," Lihua said. "But if I don't go to Changsha, if I don't at least try to find my parents, I will always wonder. I will never be able to rest knowing that I could have found them but didn't."

"Are you sure, little cub?" the timo asked. "You must know that your chances of finding them are very small. Nearly impossible."

"I...I know," Lihua said, her voice cracking. She feared she was making a mistake. But something in the back of her mind was pulling at her, telling her to keep moving. "Maybe, if I don't find them, I can come back."

The timo looked at her and gave her a sad smile. They both knew that if she left, she would never return. Still, he patted her on the shoulder anyway. "You will always be welcome here, little cub."

Lihua stood up. "I suppose I should get ready. You said it was a long journey."

The timo stood as well. "I said it was a long journey by

foot. But if you take a train, you could be there in only a couple of days."

"What's a train?" Lihua asked.

The timo smiled, and his eyes sparkled. "Well, you are in for a surprise."

CHAPTER FIFTEEN

The large black beast puffed plumes of dark smoke like an angry dragon. Even from their hiding spot well away from the train, the rumbling of the engine shook the earth beneath Lihua's feet.

"Have you ever seen anything so dreadful?" Lihua asked Panpan.

Panpan grunted and shifted on her feet. She clearly did not like the train either.

The area around the train was busy. Many people were loading the carriages up with goods. Passengers of all types were getting on and off the train. People were dressed in exotic costumes she had never seen before. There were people of different colors as well. Some had skin so pale, Lihua thought it must easily burn if it was touched by the hot sun. Other people had skin so dark, it was as black as the train. But when the black people spoke or smiled, their white teeth shined like the moon. People were rushing around selling food and other items for the long train ride.

She also saw men with guns. They weren't wearing any uniforms, but they still stood around, watching the crowd with some sort of authority. She thought that these men must work for whoever was in charge in the area. Perhaps a warlord.

Lihua reached into her bag and squeezed the small purse of coins the timo had given her. He made sure she had enough money for a train ticket and food for the journey.

Her heart beat fast in her chest as she thought about buying her ticket for the train. She feared she was making the wrong choice. The timo had been such a kind man, and the other villagers were friendly as well. They had offered her a new home. A new place in the world. They had been kind to Panpan too. And yet, she couldn't bring herself to accept. Her own parents who had raised her from a baby had rejected her. How much easier would it be for people who didn't even know her to turn her away if times got tough? Or if she didn't live up to their expectations. Or if another person—like a boy—came along? No, as kind as the timo and the other villagers had been, they were not her people. That village was not where she was meant to be. At least not yet. She had to try to find her birth parents. They were the only people who had any reason to love and accept her without condition. If she found them and they turned her away, or if she didn't find them at all, then she would find a new home. She would go back to the timo.

She knew she had to get to Changsha. Yet, she hesitated to buy her ticket. She didn't want to leave Panpan. Guilt was already gnawing in her stomach at the idea that she was going to get on that train and leave Panpan behind. But what else could she do? They wouldn't let Panpan on the train, and walking would be too far of a journey, not to mention dangerous. She'd never make it.

"Panpan," Lihua said, patting her friend on the back.

"The ticket office is right there." She pointed to a small building not far from their hiding place. "I'm just going to buy a ticket and then I'll be back, okay?"

She actually hadn't considered how she was even going to get on the train without Panpan following her, but she was taking everything one step at a time for now.

Panpan snuffled anxiously as Lihua slipped out of their hiding place, but she stayed put. Lihua gave her a reassuring smile as she slowly walked to the ticket booth and got in line.

"One ticket to Changsha," Lihua said to the man in the booth who was puffing away on a cigarette.

"What class?" the man asked.

"Umm...I don't know what you mean," Lihua said.

"First class? Second class?" the man grunted.

Lihua shook her head. "I don't know. I just need to go to Changsha."

The man sighed his annoyance. "I mean you want a hard seat? Soft seat? Bed? It's a three-day journey."

Lihua still wasn't sure what he was asking. What was a soft seat? She reached into her bag and pulled out the change purse. She handed several coins to the man.

"Whatever this will get me," she said.

The man counted the change and nodded. "Soft seat," he said. He ripped off a piece of paper, wrote something on it, then stamped it before handing it to her. "Train leaves at noon. Over there." He nodded toward the platform near the idling train.

"How long from now is that?" Lihua asked. She couldn't tell time that way.

"About fifteen minutes," the man said. "Next!" The man behind her elbowed her out of the way.

Lihua ran back to the woods and crouched in front of Panpan.

"I got a ticket," she said, and she felt a pain well up in her chest. Panpan cocked her head to the side. "I...I have to go. I can't take you on the train with me."

Panpan made a curious whine.

Lihua threw her arms around Panpan's neck. "I'll never forget you!" she said, fighting back tears.

Panpan snuffled anxiously.

"I need you to stay here," Lihua said. "Don't follow me. You might get hurt. You can go back to the bamboo forest. Find more pandas. Or maybe find another little girl who needs you."

"All aboard!" a man called from the train platform.

"Hey, little sister!" the man who sold her the ticket called out from his window. "That's your train! Don't miss it! No refunds!"

The train let out a shrill whistle.

"I have to go!" Lihua said, forcing herself to stand. She couldn't wait. And if she prolonged her goodbye, she might not be able to leave at all.

Panpan growled and nipped at Lihua's shirt, grabbing it in her mouth.

Lihua tugged at her shirt, tearing it a bit as she pulled it from Panpan's grip. "Panpan!" Lihua exclaimed, but Panpan only grunted more. "Stop it, Panpan," Lihua said, stomping her foot. "I...I..." She then turned and ran toward the train. She had to go. She couldn't look back. She knew that if she didn't leave now, she wouldn't. But she had to. She couldn't stay here for an animal.

She expected Panpan to chase after her, but as she climbed the stairs to the platform, she allowed herself a glance back at the forest. She was surprised that she didn't see Panpan anywhere, but she thought she saw a glimpse of white fur retreating into the woods. She felt a pain in her heart, but nodded her head. "Good," she mumbled.

She handed her ticket to the platform attendant, who checked it and then handed it back to her. "Car four," he said, motioning down the platform.

Lihua went to her car and looked around for Panpan one more time. When she didn't see her, she boarded the train.

Lihua was surprised to find the train car rather comfortable. It was clean and not too crowded. She used the numbers written on her ticket to find her seat, which had a cushion and a back to it. She realized the cushion was why the seat was referred to as "soft." Since it was still a seat and not a bed, she doubted she would be able to get much sleep on the journey, but it was at least better than having to travel sitting on a wooden bench. Her seat was by the window, which she eagerly looked through for Panpan.

She bit her lower lip to keep from crying when she didn't see her beloved panda. She didn't know what else she expected. Why wouldn't the panda abandon her? She wasn't a cub. It was only a matter of time before Panpan left her for her own kind anyway.

So why did she feel so heartbroken?

The train whistled again, and the last few passengers jumped onto the train as the huge beast roared to life. Lihua was tossed back as the train jutted forward. She gasped in surprise and gripped the windowsill for support. She watched as people on the platform waved goodbye to some of the passengers.

Then she heard screaming.

As the train pulled away from the platform, Lihua saw several people running along the track. She craned her neck to look back down the tracks and saw Panpan running alongside the train!

"Panpan!" she cried. She fumbled with the window to lower the glass, but she couldn't figure out the mechanism. She slapped the window with her hand and called out to her friend again.

The other passengers on the train began to crowd around the windows and talk excitedly about the panda, pointing and laughing as though it was great entertainment.

But Lihua knew it was more than that. Panpan was refusing to let her go.

Lihua's heart wrenched in her chest. She had abandoned her panda, her only friend. The only person in the world who loved her. How could she have been so cruel? Panpan had saved her life, and this was how she repaid her?

She ran to the back of the train car and went out the door onto the platform between the cars. Panpan raised her head when she saw her. Lihua waved at Panpan, then pointed to the woods. She needed to let her go. She had to get to Changsha! She had to find her mother and father. She couldn't get off the train now.

But Panpan growled and kept running alongside. The train was not moving very quickly, but it was picking up speed. Along the tracks, people were still running and screaming as Panpan approached. Behind them, she saw men with guns gathering.

Lihua waved at Panpan again. She needed to get away from the tracks and back into the woods. "No! Go! They are going to hurt you!" Lihua yelled over the wind and sounds of the train. But Panpan continued to follow alongside.

The door to the train car opened behind Lihua and a man with a gun stepped out. He took aim at Panpan.

"No!" Lihua screamed as she reached for the barrel.

They were both unsteady on the moving train, so they fell back, almost off the other side of the small platform. The man managed to catch himself. He pulled himself back up, but then pushed Lihua away from him.

"You little idiot!" he yelled.

Lihua then saw his eyes go wide, as though he didn't realize how hard he had pushed her until it was too late. But she was already falling. Falling. Falling.

She hit the ground hard, and then bounced and rolled, hitting the ground a few more times. She blacked out for a moment, and there was a ringing in her ears. But then she felt Panpan's warm tongue on her face.

"I…I'm okay," Lihua managed to choke out as she reached up and stroked Panpan's face.

She could still hear voices screaming. She looked around and saw the men with guns racing toward them. She forced herself to stand.

"Come on," she said to Panpan, and she led Panpan away from the tracks and toward the tree line. As soon as they were back in the forest, the men with guns did not follow them.

Lihua and Panpan continued on a little ways until Lihua finally collapsed. Her head was dizzy and she was in terrible pain. She vomited and then rolled onto her back.

Panpan licked Lihua's face again and whimpered.

"I'll…I'll be okay…" Lihua said, trying to comfort her friend. But as she closed her eyes, she wasn't sure she would be able to open them again.

CHAPTER SIXTEEN

When Lihua finally awoke, she was pressed up against the warm body and soft fur of Panpan. Even before she moved, though, she could feel pain in her back and neck. She then remembered her fall from the train and knew she was lucky to be alive. She opened her eyes and saw that it was dark. But whether it was the night of the same day she had fallen from the train or several nights later, she had no idea. She didn't think they had run very far from the train station. They were lucky not to have been discovered while Lihua was unconscious.

Panpan began whimpering and sniffing at Lihua's hair. She must have sensed that Lihua was awake.

Lihua reached up and petted Panpan's face. "I'm okay," she said. She forced herself to sit up. Her head spun, but she just closed her eyes and waited for it to pass.

Panpan nuzzled against Lihua's face, as if she couldn't get close enough. Lihua wrapped her arms around Panpan.

"I'm sorry, Panpan," Lihua said, fighting back tears. "I shouldn't have tried to leave you. You are the only one who has been there for me. You'd never abandon me. I can't believe I almost did that! Am I any better than Mama?"

Panpan grunted. Lihua pulled back and wiped her tears away.

"I'm here now," Lihua said. "And I'll never leave you again. I promise."

Panpan stood up and let out a happy, almost barking sound that made Lihua laugh.

"You and me, Panpan," Lihua said.

Panpan then went to tear down some bamboo stalks. If she hadn't left Lihua's side the whole time she was sleeping, she must have been quite famished. Lihua noticed she was feeling hungry as well.

She opened her bag and pulled out some of the food the timo had sent with her. Most of it had been crushed in the fall, but it was still edible. She only ate a few bites when she began to feel nauseous and light-headed, so she put the food away. She didn't want to go back to sleep, and she was feeling thirsty. She looked up and noticed the sky was already lightening. She leaned against a tree and waited for the sun to rise before they started walking again.

"If the train was going to go to Changsha," Lihua reasoned to Panpan, "then if we keep following the tracks, we will get there eventually too."

They would do their best to follow the train tracks, but also stay out of sight of any other people along the way. Lihua was surprised to see so many people traveling along the tracks. Many people were walking along the tracks like she was, using them as a guide. But other people were brave enough to jump on and off moving trains as they passed by.

Lihua realized they were doing that to ride the train for free. They weren't riding in the passenger cars like she nearly did, but were riding in storage cars.

Lihua thought that stealing a ride in a storage car was terribly dishonest. But her fingers gripped the paper ticket in her pocket. "No refunds!" the man in the ticket booth had told her, but she didn't get to actually use it. She used most of the money from the timo for her ticket but was still no closer to Changsha. If she were able to sneak back onto a train, she would only be getting the ride that was owed to her. Unfortunately, she couldn't see a way to get Panpan onto the train.

Panpan had proven herself to be a fast runner, and she was strong. But it was unlikely the bumbly, tumbly bear would be able to run fast enough and jump high enough to land inside a moving train car. If the train was sitting still, she thought Panpan still might have a difficult time getting on the train. But from what she had seen so far, the train only stopped at busy depots where there were hundreds of people around. She'd never be able to sneak a panda onto a train at a station.

Lihua sighed in disappointment as they walked. She was going to be an old woman by the time she found her parents, if ever. How long had she even been traveling so far? She had no idea. But what choice did she have? For days, Lihua and Panpan did their best to follow the train tracks from the safety of the woods, ever so slowly continuing toward their goal.

"Did you hear that?" Lihua asked Panpan in the dark. She sat up and looked around, certain she had heard voices. Panpan lifted her head and sniffed the air, pointing her nose in one direction. Lihua sniffed as well and smelled smoke. Someone must have been camping nearby.

"We should go," Lihua whispered as she gathered up their few things. She started to walk deeper into the woods, but Panpan headed toward the smoke and voices.

"No, Panpan," Lihua whispered harshly. "What are you doing?" But there was no stopping Panpan, so Lihua followed silently behind her.

Just as Lihua feared, they came upon a camp of fellow train followers. She had seen them walking along the day previously. They had stood out to her from the rest because they appeared to be a family group: an elderly husband and wife, their two grown sons and their wives, and several children. While Lihua had seen many women traveling along with the men, this group was unique because of the children. They were all sitting around a large fire.

"I'm hungry, Mama," one of the little girls whined.

"Eat your mushrooms," her mother said.

"They taste yucky!" a little boy said.

"It's all we have," the boy's father snapped.

"Once we get to the city, everything will be better," the oldest man said.

The family then settled into an uneasy silence.

Lihua wondered if the family was also heading to Changsha. They mentioned going to a city, and it was the only city she knew of. She sat in the safety of the dark for a long while. Part of her wanted to talk to them. Maybe ask if they could travel together. It would be safer to travel in a group. They said they had mushrooms. She didn't know how to forage for mushrooms. Maybe they could teach her. She could give them some huajiao in exchange.

It was probably stupid and dangerous, but she decided to try and talk to them. After all, Panpan had decided to approach the camp instead of sneaking deeper into the woods. She probably sensed some good in these people.

"H-h-hello?" Lihua finally called out from her hiding spot.

"Who's there?" the men asked, jumping up and brandishing sticks as weapons.

"I'm no one," Lihua said. "Just a girl with her p—. Her pet. Can I share your fire?"

"It sounds like a child," one of the women whispered to the group.

"Could be a trap," one of the men said.

"I'm the only person here," Lihua said, hoping to reassure them. "I'm trying to travel to Changsha."

The family exchanged more looks and shrugs. The men finally lowered their weapons.

"Okay, girl," the family patriarch said. "Come on out, but slowly."

Lihua held up her hands as she stood and stepped forward into the light of the fire.

The whole family seemed to visibly relax when they saw that she was who she claimed to be.

"Make sure there is no one else back there," the father told one of his sons.

"Wait," Lihua said. "My...my pet. She's going to come out now. But don't be afraid. She won't hurt you."

"Is it a dog?" asked one of the little girls? "I like dogs."

Lihua smiled, still holding up her hands. "No, she's not a dog. She's better than a dog. Come on out, Panpan."

The family gasped as Panpan emerged from the forest.

"Is that—?"

"By the gods!"

"Wow! Neat!"

The family was at once shocked, excited, and afraid as the panda stepped nearer to the fire.

Lihua kneeled down by Panpan's side and hugged her. "See, she won't hurt you."

The adults all shook their heads, but the kids jumped up and ran to the panda at once.

"Is it a real panda?" one of them asked.

"It must be a costume," one of the others said.

"Maybe it's a fairy!" another one exclaimed.

The adults all stood and stared in shock.

"Who are you?" the old mother finally asked Lihua.

Lihua shrugged. "As I said, I'm nobody. I have no home. No family. I was kidnapped from my home in Changsha as a baby. At least, I think I was kidnapped. I don't really know. I'm trying to get back there so I can find my birth parents."

The older couple shook their heads and sat down, motioning for Lihua to join them.

"Such a tragedy," the old man said. "This is not uncommon. Some families are so desperate for a child, they will do anything to get one. Even stealing one from another family."

"My grandmother said my parents bought be from a man who had many children for sale," Lihua explained.

The old woman nodded her head. "Traffickers. They are like poachers of children. Snatching them anywhere they can and selling them down the road."

"Do parents...sell their children to traffickers?" Lihua asked, not sure she wanted to know the answer.

"Sometimes," the old woman said. "When a family is poor, they sometimes will do that. But in that case, they usually sell the child to someone they know. Even the most desperate of parents want to know their children are safe."

As tragic as the old woman's words were, there was a ring of hope to them for Lihua. If her birth parents had sold her, it most likely wouldn't have been to a trafficker. She probably had been kidnapped. Her birth parents would be thrilled for her to return. She felt warmth bubble up in her chest once again.

"Mama," one of the little girls said once the novelty of Panpan wore off. "I'm still hungry."

"I'm sorry, little one," the mother said, pulling her child close and rocking her. "Just try to sleep, then you won't feel hungry."

"I might be able to help with that," Lihua said. "If your sons can chop down some bamboo stalks and gather some water, I can cook for you. I heard you say you had mushrooms."

"You can cook?" the old woman asked, surprised. "Here on the road?"

"My parents...I mean, the people who bought me, they had a small restaurant in our village," Lihua said.

The family nodded their approval and gathered around the fire. Once the men brought the supplies she needed, she got to work making her bamboo hotpot. The food was quickly fragrant as she dropped the huajiao into the water and bamboo concoction. The family eagerly looked forward to the meal.

When the food was done and Lihua helped hand around the bamboo tubes of food, the family barely waited until it was cool before digging in. Lihua wondered how long it had been since they had eaten a decent supper.

"It's so spicy!" one of the boys said with a laugh.

"My lips are tingling!" said one of the girls.

"This is very good," one of the young mothers said. "You will have to teach me how to cook this way."

"If you let me travel with you to Changsha," said Lihua, "I can cook for you every night, and give you whatever huajiao peppers I have left when we part ways."

"We would be happy to have you travel with us, little one," the patriarch said. "But we will be hopping onto a train soon. Can your panda get on a train?"

"That's what I was afraid of," Lihua said with a sigh. "That's why I'm walking and not taking a train right now. I can't leave Panpan."

Panpan rolled on her back, happily munching her bamboo.

"But if we can get on at the junction," said one of the women, "surely the panda can as well."

"What is the junction?" Lihua asked.

"Not far from here, the rail line splits," the patriarch explained. "It continues east to Changsha or splits north to Wuhan. For a few minutes, the train will stop so the railwaymen can switch from one line to another. It's not a proper station, so there are not many people around. But it is a good place for people who can't jump on the train elsewhere—like the children—to try and board."

"Panpan is fast and strong," Lihua said. "If the train stops, I'm sure she could get on."

The family all happily agreed to the plan.

"You'll need to get off the train before Changsha, though," the old man went on. "Changsha is a big city with a busy station. If you ride it into Changsha, you will surely be caught."

"Just tell me when we need to get off the train and we will," Lihua said. "Thank you so much for your help."

"Welcome to our family of vagabonds," one of the sons said, and the family laughed.

"Why are you traveling?" Lihua asked. "Where is your home."

"Our home was destroyed," the old mother said. "The whole village burned down by warlords."

"That's terrible," Lihua said.

"But in Changsha, there is hope," one of the sons said. "The communists, they are building a new world for all of us."

"The communists?" Lihua asked. She had heard the word before, but she had no idea what it meant.

"Since the empress's death, the whole country has been in chaos," the other son said. "No stability. No hope. Only fighting."

"It was still peaceful where I lived," Lihua said. "But I have heard about the wars on my travels."

"Don't worry, little one," the old father said. "Whatever happens with your parents, whether you find them or not, there will be no better place for you in China than in Changsha."

Lihua wasn't sure about that, but she hoped he was right.

CHAPTER SEVENTEEN

Lihua and Panpan traveled with the family—who she found out was the Luo family—for the next couple of days toward the junction where they hoped to sneak aboard the train. Even though the family could have more easily traveled along the tracks, they stuck to the woods out of consideration for Lihua and Panpan. Lihua gave the family the little money she had left to buy some food in a village they passed by, and Lihua helped the family forage for food in the woods. Panpan happily helped the family pull down more stalks of bamboo than they could ever eat. One of the women helped show Lihua how to find mushrooms and explained which types were good for eating and which were poisonous. When they finally stopped traveling in the evenings, Lihua added some of her precious huajiao peppercorns to their meals, which the whole family—but especially the children—enjoyed immensely.

Lihua tried not to feel sorry for herself as she watched the family work together and dream of the new life they would have once they reached Changsha. As much as her heart still hurt over the loss of her adoptive family, she missed them. She missed working with them and running the noodle shop. She missed helping her mother harvest and dry the peppercorns. She missed helping her father prepare the tubes of bamboo rice. She missed not worrying about the future but dreaming of the day her mother would help her prepare for her own marriage and family.

And she missed her grandmother. She missed praying with her and hearing the stories of the gods and ancestors. She missed her warm smile and the gentle way she would touch her cheek as she fell asleep.

She even missed the litter brother she never got a chance to know.

They weren't perfect, but they were her family. She would have done anything they asked if they would have allowed her to stay. As she watched the Luo family, she could tell that they had been through hard times, but they had persevered together. Their love was strong, not just because they were related by blood—after all, the daughters had married in—but because of what they had all been through together.

Yet, if Lihua asked them if she could just stay with them, she suspected they would accept her, but doubted they would welcome her into the fold so completely.

It was similar to how she felt at the timo's village. Yes, he was kind to her, and he would have let her stay, but he wasn't her family.

But, if she found her birth family, would they accept her so readily? They didn't know her, and she didn't know them. Would blood be a strong enough bond to repair the years of separation?

She was so confused. She didn't have the blood to be

family to her adoptive parents. She didn't have the family history to be accepted by her birth family.

Would she ever really find her home?

Late at night, while the family would sleep huddled together near the fire, wives with husbands, children with parents, Lihua slept snuggled in the warm fur of Panpan. She knew that the only real family she had—one that was stronger than history, or blood, or even species—was Panpan. And yet she had nearly abandoned her at the train station. The guilt over that near-choice still haunted her daily. And while she knew Panpan had forgiven her, she doubted she would ever be able to forgive herself.

Finally, late in the afternoon on the third day, they came to where the tracks split. There was no train in sight, but she noticed several other people milling about in the area as well. Most of them were old, missing a limb, had a limp, or had small children with them.

Lihua, Panpan, and the Luo family stayed hidden in the woods as they watched the track.

"There's no train," Lihua said. "What do we do?"

"We have to wait," the old man said. "Eventually, a train will come, and the engineer and his men will get out to switch the track. That is when we will get on the train."

"There are too many people around," one of the sons said. "The engineer and his men must know that this is a popular area for people to try and board the train. Surely they will be watching. What if we are caught?"

"We will have to be quick and quiet," the father said. "We must avoid the other groups of people. Have the smaller children strapped to your backs and ready to go."

Lihua sat quietly and listened to the plans, her heart thumping in her chest. She had no idea if Panpan would be able to board the train quickly or quietly. She remembered that the railwaymen back at the train station had guns. She didn't want to put the Luo family at risk after all they had done to help her.

"I think you all should board the next train without us," Lihua said. "Panpan and I will wait here and catch a later train."

"But how will you know when to get off the train?" the old father asked.

Lihua hadn't considered that. "I will just keep watch and we will get off before we get to Changsha."

The family all looked at one another and shook their heads.

"No," one of the sons said firmly, placing his hand on Lihua's shoulder. "We will all go together."

Lihua exhaled in relief and did her best not to cry. She didn't really want to separate from the Luos, but she wanted to do what was best. She was happy they were not ready to say goodbye to her just yet.

It was late at night when a train finally came to a stop at the junction. It was a long train that extended farther than Lihua could see in the dark. She was surprised to see that many of the train cars had open doors, including one right across from where the family was hiding. Lihua, Panpan, and the Luo family all held their breaths as they waited to see what the railwaymen and the other people hoping to hop onto the train would do.

Just as they suspected, several men got off the train and headed to the junction to switch the tracks, but other men —men with guns—began to patrol the train. And worse, as they heard the sound of barking, they knew the men had dogs with them as well.

"Dogs!" The old mother gasped. "They are sure to smell us if we try to board the train!"

They watched from the woods as the men with dogs went from car to car. They didn't enter every train car, but if the dogs sensed anything suspicious, they would growl, and the men would board the car. Sometimes they emerged with nothing, but other times they would exit the car, kicking a vagrant out and running him off by threatening him with the guns and with a dog snapping at his heels.

"We will wait until they pass," the old father said. "Then we will board the train. Hopefully they won't check the cars twice."

"But the dogs—" the old mother tried to protest, but her husband cut her off.

"What other choice do we have?"

"Hey! Stop!" they heard a man yell. They watched as a railwayman and his dog ran toward people who were trying to board the train several cars down. The dog barked and a woman screamed. They heard a gunshot and more screaming.

"We should go while the men are distracted," the old father said.

His wife looked at him like he was crazy, but she knew she didn't have a choice. She had to obey her husband, and somehow, the family had to get to Changsha.

The family, Lihua, and Panpan huddled near the edge of the woods. Lihua's heart beat so hard she could feel it in her nose. She couldn't believe what they were about to do. And Panpan! If the dogs could smell people, surely, they could smell a panda as well. There was no chance they weren't going to get caught.

"Go!" the old man said harshly.

The whole family broke into a run. Lihua didn't even look to see where the railwaymen were, she just looked ahead at the train car with the open door. They all reached the car at about the same time. As quickly as they could, the Luo family jumped into the car, the younger members helping the older ones and then everyone on the train helping to pull up the people who were carrying the children.

One of the men grabbed Lihua's hand and easily lifted her into the train car. She looked back to see if Panpan needed help. She gasped when she saw that Panpan was not even attempting to climb into the train, but had stopped to pee around the door!

"Panpan!" Lihua whispered harshly, her voice higher pitched than she meant it to be. "Come on! Let's go!" But Panpan seemed unconcerned as she continued to empty her bladder around the door and on the car's wheels.

"We need to hide," one of the women said.

"That panda's going to give us away!" someone else exclaimed. One of the children began to cry.

The family became frantic as they scrambled behind crates and under tarps to try and hide in case the railwaymen searched the car on their way back to the engine. Not that hiding would keep the dogs from smelling them, especially now that Panpan had peed all over the outside of the car. The dogs were sure to smell her!

Lihua was about to jump off the train and run back into the woods when Panpan gripped the edge of the train car opening and easily hauled herself up into the car. Lihua led Panpan behind a stack of boxes in the back of the car. Everyone held their breath as they heard the railwaymen making their way back up the track and the yipping of their dogs as they sniffed the cars.

When he railwaymen got to the car Lihua and the others were hiding in, she could hear the dogs sniff the outside of the car.

"What is it, boy?" his handler asked. The dog let out a whimper, and then he and his handler moved on.

Only a few moments later, the train whistle blew and they felt the train jerk forward as it started to move again.

"We're alive!" The old mother said in shock as they all ventured out of their hiding places. Surprisingly, they weren't the only people hiding on the train car.

"Well I'll be darned," said another vagrant when he saw Panpan. Eventually, half a dozen more people emerged from hiding spots.

"I think the dogs were scared of the panda smell," one of the young men said.

The old man patted Lihua on the back and then rubbed Panpan behind the ears. "Your panda might have just saved us all," he said.

Lihua felt a sense of pride well up in her chest as she hugged Panpan. Everyone laughed and clapped, thankful for the girl and her panda.

For the next few days, anytime the train stopped at night, Panpan would get out of the train car and pee around the door and wheels. The dogs never stopped in front of their car. As such, their little community of travelers grew as more and more people hopped into the car the dogs were avoiding. They couldn't make a fire to cook any food, but the travelers all shared what little they had, and no one went hungry.

Panpan was the hero of the train car, and everyone wanted to pet and kiss the lucky panda who had saved their lives. They all wanted to know everything about the Lihua and Panpan and their incredible journey.

"I don't know if Panpan is a fairy," an older woman told Lihua, "but she is certainly your guardian spirit. She wouldn't let you leave her because she knew you had more important work to do together."

"If you had tried to travel on without her," a man added, "something bad probably would have happened to you."

"Maybe she is an ancestor spirit from your birth family," one of the little Luo girls said.

"Or one from your adoptive family," someone else chimed in. "Atoning for the cruel way your parents treated you."

Speculation about who Panpan really was never ended, and while Lihua would be happy just knowing that Panpan was nothing more than a regular old panda, it was fun to hear the elaborate stories the other people came up with about her.

But finally, her train journey was coming to its end.

"You need to get off the train at the next stop," the old man told Lihua. "After that, the train will pull into Changsha, right in the middle of the city. It would be too dangerous for you to try to get off the train there."

"How far will I be from Changsha?" Lihua asked.

"Only a day's walk," he said.

Lihua nodded and fought back the tears that pricked at her eyes. Even though she had only known the Luos and the rest of the train riders a few days, she had felt like a part of a community, and she was sad to leave them.

"Changsha might feel like a big city at first," the old man said. "But I think the world is really a very small place. We will see each other again, little sister."

Lihua certainly hoped so.

She could feel the train slowing under her, and everyone crowded around her and Panpan to see them off. She slung her bag over her shoulders, and everyone put a little something—food, matches, incense, whatever they could spare—into it.

"It is daytime," the old man said. "It will be impossible for you to get off the train without being seen. All you can do is jump off the train and run into the woods as fast as your feet can carry you. Don't look back."

Lihua nodded as she felt the train slow down even more. She and Panpan both stood at the ready by the open door. Lihua worried her lower lip as she leaned out and looked at the station they were approaching. It wasn't as big as the station she had originally tried to board at, but there were still a lot of people around. The man was right, they would certainly be seen. She just had to hope that even if they were spotted, that the railwaymen wouldn't try to pursue them...or shoot them. Over the last few days, she had no idea how many people the railwaymen had killed as they inspected the train at every stop. She knew sometimes they only fired warning shots. But based on the screams she had heard, sometimes the railway guards did hit their targets.

Panpan grunted nervously as the train slowed to a stop. The wheels had not even stopped grinding when Lihua and Panpan leaped from the train and hit the ground at a run. She heard many shocked gasps and yelps from people at the station who caught sight of them.

"Hey! Stop!" Lihua heard someone yell, but she didn't stop, and she didn't look back.

"Holy...Is that a...?" she heard someone else call out.

Panpan growled, but they both kept running toward the tree line. They heard some dogs bark, and then the sound of a gunshot, but they kept running. Even after they reached the forest, they didn't stop. Lihua's heart was beating rapidly, and her lungs were burning like they were on fire. She feared that if she stopped to catch her breath, she wouldn't be able to start running again, so they ran as far and fast as they could. They ran until they could no longer see the train or the tracks or hear the many voices of the people riding the train and working at the station. They ran until she heard the train whistle blow, signaling that it was pulling out of the station and heading for Changsha. Only then, did she finally stop to breathe, and Panpan stopped with her.

"We...we did it, Panpan," Lihua said as she collapsed and rubbed Panpan's ears. "We made it! By this time tomorrow, we'll be home!"

CHAPTER EIGHTEEN

"Come on, Panpan!" Lihua exclaimed as they ran through the woods in the direction of Changsha. Lihua's heart was full to bursting, and she could not contain her excitement. Tomorrow, everything would change. Everything would be different. She couldn't believe she had come so far and was so near her goal. She finally began to let herself dream.

"What do you think Mama is like?" she asked Panpan. "I'll bet she's beautiful. With the longest flowing hair. Every night, she'll let me brush it until it shines in the moonlight. Perhaps she'll brush mine too."

Panpan grunted as she trotted along to keep up with Lihua.

"Oh, don't worry," Lihua said. "Human hair is certainly not as beautiful as panda fur. No one is more beautiful than you."

Panpan growled her acceptance of this.

"I hope she's a good cook," Lihua went on as she leaped over fallen branches. "I wonder what food is like in Changsha. Probably not as flavorful as what we had back home.

Good thing I still have some huajiao peppercorns left. And what about Baba? What do you think he's like? My other baba was so quiet and worked all the time. I didn't know him at all. Maybe my new baba will—"

She froze, certain she heard something. Panpan stopped and sniffed the air.

"You heard it too?" Lihua asked. Lihua crouched down and listened. There it was again, she was sure of it. A child crying.

"I'm sure it's nothing," Lihua said to Panpan as she stood back up. "Probably another traveling family..."

Panpan grunted as they heard the crying again. But this time, Lihua thought she heard two children. She turned toward the sounds and realized they were coming from deeper in the woods, in a direction away from Changsha.

"We...we should keep going," Lihua said. "It will be dark soon anyway..."

Panpan nudged Lihua's hand, and Lihua felt a tugging at her heart when she heard more crying.

Lihua sighed. As anxious as she was to get to Changsha, she couldn't just leave a child—or children—in the forest. What if they were lost? Or injured?

"Come on," Lihua said, even though she was dragging her own heels. "Changsha isn't going anywhere."

They walked carefully and quietly toward the sounds, and Lihua grew more anxious as she realized she could hear the cries of several children. Then the voices of men.

"Shut up," one man said.

"Get a move on," said another.

Lihua's heart beat rapidly in her chest as she and Panpan peeked around a tree and saw two men escorting at least half a dozen children through the woods. The children looked nothing alike and were of varying ages. The oldest looked to be about six years old, but two babies were being carried strapped to the men's backs.

"Traffickers," Lihua grumbled to Panpan.

"I want Mama," one little girl who looked to be about four cried.

"Be quiet and keep going," one of the men barked as he pushed the little girl forward.

Lihua felt a rage in her chest at the rough way the man handled the child. Was this what it was like when she had been taken from her family? Her grandmother had said that the man who sold her had many children with him. Even though she knew what had happened to her, seeing it still happening to more children made her angry and sad. She wanted to do something, but what?

Lihua and Panpan followed the group from a safe distance while Lihua tried to come up with a plan. But eventually, she noticed that the men carried guns with them. When she saw the guns, she froze and crouched on the ground. Panpan grunted and nudged her to keep walking, but Lihua held her back.

"No," Lihua said. "They have guns! They could easily kill us both. Then what? This whole journey will have been for nothing. We should leave. Go to Changsha. We can tell someone what we saw. Let people know that the children are alive and the direction the traffickers went. Then their families can come after them."

Panpan grunted angrily and nudged Lihua back in the direction the traffickers were taking the children, but Lihua held her ground.

"No!" Lihua said. "I'm so close! My parents, I know they are waiting for me! I've come so far..." Tears welled up in her eyes. "I just want to go home!"

"I wanna go home!" one of the children cried, his voice echoing through the woods.

"Shut up, you little brat!" one of the men yelled. Then Lihua heard a slapping sound, and the children started crying again.

Lihua's face burned and she clenched her fists. She felt an anger boil in her stomach she had never felt before.

For the first time, she let herself feel angry. Angry at her adoptive parents for abandoning her. For never loving her as they should. For buying her in the first place. Anger at her grandmother for not fighting for her. Anger at the ancestors for not protecting her. Anger at her birth parents for losing her.

But mostly anger at the traffickers who caught and sold her like a fish at the market.

She had suffered so much. Lost everything. Her body ached from her journey and her heart ached from loss. She didn't know how she would ever recover from what she had experienced. All she knew was that she couldn't let more children suffer the way she had. She had to do something to save those children and return them home.

"Fine," Lihua said to Panpan. "Let's do something to help those children."

Panpan snuffled and they continued following the men and the children. When they caught up with them, all of the children were crying and the men were frustrated.

"Let's camp here," one of the men said. "Maybe they'll stop crying."

"Fine," the other man grunted as he untied the baby from his back and handed it to the six-year-old. "All of you, sit down and shut up or I'll give you something to cry about."

The children all sighed in relief at being able to sit

down. For such little ones, a day's walk must have seemed like forever.

"You stand guard while I find water," one man ordered the other.

"Right," the man said, and he removed the child from his back, placing it in a basket, and then holding up his gun as he looked out into the woods.

Lihua leaned back behind her tree and shook her head at Panpan. "What are we going to do about those guns?"

Panpan grunted as she looked up at the sky. Lihua looked up as well. It was getting close to evening, and the first star was already twinkling.

"We will have to wait until dark," Lihua said. "Darkness will be our only hope."

CHAPTER NINETEEN

Little pearl.

Lihua opened her eyes. Had she fallen asleep? How could she? Where were the children? Where was Panpan?

Little pearl.

She gasped and turned around. She had heard something.

"Who's there?" she whispered, then she gasped when a woman with long white hair and wearing a black fur wrap turned around and smiled at her.

"Hello, little pearl," the woman said.

"Nainai!" Lihua exclaimed as she ran into her grandmother's arms. All the anger and despair she felt before melted away as she fell into the familiar, safe embrace. "I've missed you!"

Nainai held Lihua tight and ran her hand over her granddaughter's head and down her hair. "And I you, little pearl."

"But what are you doing here?" Lihua asked. "How did you find me?"

"You have forgotten the old ways," her grandmother said. "When was the last time you prayed to the ancestors?"

"I prayed at every temple I found," Lihua said. But then she realized that it had been quite a while since she last found one. Days, weeks even? She had stopped looking for them. Lihua dropped her head shamefully. "I'm sorry."

Nainai chuckled and hugged Lihua again. "Do not be sad. Tonight is very special."

"What is tonight?" Lihua asked, but Nainai simply raised her eyes to the night sky.

Lihua looked up and saw that the moon was full. That was when she remembered what day it was.

"Ghost Festival," Lihua said. Then she looked at her grandmother with her eyes wide. "Are you a....Did you...?"

Nainai nodded. "Many weeks ago. I think part of my spirit flew out of me and followed you when you left. There was not enough left to sustain me."

"Nainai," Lihua cried. "I'm so sorry."

"Don't say that," Nainai said. "I would much rather be here with you than stuck with that witch of a daughter-in-law for years on end."

"My mother..." Lihua said, but she couldn't quite bring herself to ask about her parents. Whether they were glad she was gone or regretted sending her away, what did it matter now?

Nainai shook her head. "Do not concern yourself with them," she said. "That part of your life is over."

"Then what now?" Lihua asked. "What happens to me now?"

"I don't know," Nainai said. "I only came to tell you not to fear, and to never lose your faith. The ancestors will always guide you."

"Which ancestors?" Lihua asked. "I still don't know who my family is."

"That is why I came to you today," Nainai said. "Today, we are all one family."

Lihua felt a fullness in her heart. Even though she had lost her birth family and her adoptive family, there were still people in this world—living and dead—who loved and protected her. Unlike other festivals to venerate a family's ancestors, Ghost Festival was a night to celebrate all ancestors. Those who were loved, those who were forgotten, those who crossed your path for only a moment, or those you spent your whole life with. Lihua thought about all the wonderful people she had met on her journey. The elderly nun. The timo. The Luo family. Her grandmother.

Panpan.

"Panpan," Lihua said, looking around. "Where is she?"

"She is right where you need her to be," Nainai said. "As she always has been."

Lihua opened her eyes and realized she was snuggled up against Panpan's thick fur. She looked up at the night sky and saw the moon—round and full and nearly as bright as the sun—shining down on them.

It had only been a dream. But a dream full of meaning. She was angry, yes. But she would use that anger to save the other children. But she wouldn't let her anger consume her. She had many wonderful people in her life to be thankful for.

And she had Panpan.

Her dream had certainly been right about that. Panpan

was always by her side, and together they would find a way to rescue the children from the traffickers.

She had forgotten that tonight was Ghost Festival, but she knew there had to be a way to use the festival to her advantage.

She peeked back into the camp the traffickers had made. The men were lounging around the fire, chewing on bits of a rabbit one of them had caught and roasted. The children were all huddled together on one side of the fire, their eyes wide, too scared to sleep.

Panpan shifted on her feet, and a twig snapped.

"What was that?" one of the men asked as he sat up straight, holding his gun tight.

"What was what?" the other asked lazily.

"I heard something," the nervous man said.

"Just a squirrel," the other said.

"I told you we shouldn't have done this tonight," the man said, his eyes still darting around. "We should have waited until after the festival."

"Yeah, yeah," the first man said. "Then another festival would have come, then another one. It never ends. You're just making excuses."

"No, no," the nervous man said. "It's Ghost Festival. There is no boundary between the living and the dead. Angry ghosts are sure to find us."

"By the gods, will you shut up," the other man said. "Superstitious nonsense! Now go to sleep. We have a long journey ahead. Have to get as far away from the city as possible before we can find a buyer for the brats."

The men quieted down, but Lihua had a feeling the nervous man wasn't going to sleep a wink. But it didn't matter. The fact that he was already afraid was enough. She smiled at Panpan. She had an idea.

Lihua knew that one of the men had found a creek nearby when he went looking for supplies for the evening because he had come back with fresh water. She and Panpan found the stream easily. Lihua went to the water's edge and gathered up some mud, which she then slathered all over herself and over the white portions of Panpan's fur. She then pulled the last of her joss sticks out of her bag and lit them. There was nearly a dozen left, so when they were all lit together, they gave off impressive sparks and smoke. Lihua climbed up on Panpan's back and held the joss sticks up in both of her hands.

"Ready, Panpan?" Lihua asked.

Panpan growled.

"Let's go!"

Panpan let out a ferocious roar and Lihua screamed like she was being murdered as Panpan galloped through the woods toward the camp.

They made such a racket that the men were already on their feet as Panpan crashed through the last of the brush and into the dying light of the campfire.

Lihua wailed. "You have dishonored me!"

Both the men yelled in fright and the children screamed.

"Leave or die!" Lihua wailed while Panpan roared again.

One of the men ran off instantly. The other raised his gun and fired. Lihua flinched, but the shot went well over her head.

"You have chosen death!" she screamed, and Panpan lunged toward the man.

The man yelled, dropped his gun, and fled into the forest.

Lihua wanted to laugh, both because the men's reactions were hilarious and because she was in shock that her plan worked, but she knew she mustn't waste time. She and Panpan needed to get the children to safety in case the men returned.

She jumped down off of Panpan and went to the children, who were all crying inconsolably.

"Everything is okay," Lihua said as she did her best to wipe the mud from her face. "I'm not a ghost. I'm here to help you."

"I want Mama!" One of the children said.

"Okay!" Lihua said with a smile. "Let's go find Mama."

The children slowly stopped crying and let Lihua prepare them for the journey back to Changsha.

The younger children climbed on Panpan's back and held the basket with the babies. The two older children each took one of Lihua's hands and they all left the camp together.

CHAPTER TWENTY

Traveling with the children turned out to be much harder than Lihua had anticipated. Thankfully, she had Panpan with her, and after traveling with the Luos' children, she knew they had to stop often.

At first, she was scared that the traffickers would come to their senses and chase after them, so she pushed the children to travel as fast as possible. But they wore out quickly, leading to tears and tantrums, both of which slowed them down and made a lot of noise.

After they had traveled for several hours, Panpan finally stopped walking and grunted at Lihua.

"Fine," Lihua said. "We will rest."

She didn't want to make a fire, though, for fear the light and smoke would attract attention. She found some raw carrots in her bag that some of the other train riders must have put there, and she gave them to the children who were old enough to eat solid food. In the baskets with the babies, she found some jars of milk the men must have put there. Lihua and the oldest girl fed the two babies.

Panpan gathered leaves and branches and made a small

nest. One by one, the children climbed into the nest and fell asleep with Panpan. Lihua stayed awake, though, to keep watch over the children and listen for any signs the men might have followed them.

She realized that if she had left Panpan at the train station, she never would have come across the traffickers and had the chance to save the children. Right now, those children would be lost from their families forever. Somehow, Panpan knew that they had to stick together. That even though traveling together would be more difficult, it was the right path to take.

As Lihua watched the children sleeping soundly—safe, with full bellies, and knowing they would see their parents again—Lihua felt oddly at peace. The journey had been hard, but rescuing these children had been worth it. She wondered if there was some way she could keep doing this sort of work when she grew up.

Traveling with the children was much slower than traveling with only Panpan. The children could not walk as fast and had to rest often. She had only been a day's journey from Changsha when she got off the train, but with the children, they did not see the outskirts of the city until four days later.

Even from the cover of the woods, Changsha was unlike anything Lihua had seen before. Hundreds of carts and thousands of people were traveling along wide paved roads past huge buildings made of stone. Lihua's mouth went dry as she suddenly wondered how she could possibly find her parents among so many people.

At first, she wasn't sure what to do with the children.

She couldn't leave them with just anyone. But then she saw a man in a military uniform walk by holding a gun. If anyone were in a position of authority who could help her, it would be a man like that.

"Panpan," Lihua said. "Stay here with the children. I'll be right back."

Lihua ran after the man and told him she needed help. She asked him to follow her, and he did.

"Don't be shocked," she warned him. When he saw the panda standing guard over the children, his jaw dropped. But what he said next shocked Lihua even more.

"You're the girl with the panda!" he exclaimed.

"You...you've heard of me?" she asked.

"My auntie," he said. "She arrived a few days ago on a train from the west. She said there was a girl on her train traveling with a panda. We didn't believe her! Thought she must have lost her mind. But you are real....and you are here!"

"Finally," Lihua said. "It has been a long journey. Will you be able to help the children find their way home?"

"We will do our best," he said. "They haven't been missing long, but kidnappers and traffickers have been rampant. I'll take them to party headquarters. See what we can do."

"Party headquarters?" Lihua asked.

"The Communist Party Headquarters," the man said, his chest puffing up with pride. "We are in charge around here, and we make sure every person is taken care of when they join the party."

Lihua was intrigued.

"Can children join?" she asked.

"If you are old enough to work, the party will have you," he said. "Do you want to come with me to sign up?"

"Not just yet," Lihua said. "I need to try and find my parents. But if I don't..." She didn't want to commit to anything, but if she found herself without any other option, maybe the communists would take her in.

"What are their names?" the man asked. "If they are party members, we can help you find them."

Lihua shook her head. "I don't know," she said, pulling out her silver bracelet. "I was kidnapped as a baby. All I have is this bracelet. The man who sold me said I was from Changsha, but that would have been many years ago."

"Can I see it?" the man asked, reaching for her bracelet. Lihua handed it to him. He looked at it closely, examining it in the light. "These are numbers, your birth date." Lihua nodded. "Kaifu District. Not far from here. Just head north. The other characters are the silversmith's signature. If you go to the artisan street, you might find him. Maybe he will remember something." He handed her the bracelet back.

"Thank you!" Lihua said, excitement building in her stomach. She was so close! She hugged each of the children, and they all hugged her and Panpan before the soldier finally led them away.

"I can't wait to tell my aunt what happened today!" he said with a laugh. "She's going to think I'm the crazy one now!"

Lihua shook her head. It was incredible that the one person she had asked for help in a city like this was one who had heard of her.

Lihua and Panpan headed toward Kaifu District, sticking to wooded areas when they could, but slipping down quiet alleys when they had to. When they made it to the artisan street, Lihua hid Panpan behind a stack of crates where she could keep an eye on her as she spoke to some of the craftspeople. The first silversmith she spoke to recognized the signature immediately and pointed her to another booth where an older man was polishing a new bracelet very similar to her own.

"Hello?" she asked as she approached him, holding her bracelet out. "Did you make this?"

He took the bracelet and glanced at it quickly. "Seems so," he said. "What of it? I don't do buybacks, if that's what you're after. You'll have to sell it at another shop."

"No," Lihua said, shaking her head. "I was wondering...hoping, maybe, that you might remember it, or my parents. I was kidnapped as a baby and this is all I have to find them."

The man looked up at her and pressed his lips into a thin line. "Sorry to hear that," he said. "Bad business, stealing kids. Happens more often than you'd like to think. But I make dozens of bracelets a week for new kids. And this must be, what? At least nine, ten years ago? Sorry, little sister. I wouldn't know which family purchased this bracelet in particular."

Lihua's heart fell hard in her chest and her hands started to shake. "Th-thanks for your time..." she mumbled as she turned away.

"Wait," the old silversmith called out to her. "There...there might be something."

"Yes?" Lihua asked. "Anything! The smallest chance would be more than I have now."

He nodded solemnly. "There is a wall not far from here. They call it maleiqiang, mother's tear wall. When a child goes missing, the parents will put a notice up on the wall. Not much, just dates and names. But..."

"Thank you!" Lihua said. "Where is it?"

"Back down the alley," he said, pointing. "Follow to the end and turn right. Keep going. You won't miss it."

"Thank you! Thank you!" Lihua exclaimed as she ran back to Panpan's hiding place. Together, they wound their way back down the alley to the maleiqiang.

The silversmith had been right. The maleiqiang was impossible to miss. The long wall was at least eight feet tall and crumbling in some places. It looked like it used to be a protective outer wall of the city, but as the city's boundaries expanded, the wall was neglected and allowed to decay, withered away by wind, rain, and people who secreted the bricks away to build their own homes.

But the saddest thing about the wall was that it was covered in hundreds, if not thousands, of fliers for missing children.

The fliers were little more than yellowed pieces of paper with black writing on them. Some of the fliers looked new, while others were so worn the writing could no longer be read. Lihua looked up at the clouds that were developing as the evening came and thought about the countless fliers that must have been lost with every rainstorm.

Each flier had the same basic information on it. A child's name, gender, and birthdate, along with the names of the parents and where they could be found. For many of the children, that was where the flier ended, but some parents added a bit more information. If a child had an identifying birthmark or mole, that was included. Some said where the child had last been seen or the clothes they had been wearing. A few included a rough sketch of the child, but Lihua doubted the children actually looked like the crude images. But, no matter how detailed or limited the words on the fliers, each one was a painful story of devastating loss.

There was no one around as Lihua and Panpan scanned the wall. "I don't know how I'd be able to find my flier in all this," Lihua said sadly, if a flier had ever been put up for her at all. She wondered how many cities had walls just like this, and how many children went missing who were never put on a wall. The pain each of these separated families weighed in her heart like a stone.

Panpan nudged Lihua toward the wall, and Lihua nodded.

"You're right," Lihua said as she looked back up the wall. "We've come too far to give up now. If I have to read every single flier to find one that sounds like it could be mine, then that's just what I'll have to do."

Panpan grunted and looked further down the wall. Two women had approached the wall and were kneeling at it, as though asking for the wall's blessing. They had put some joss sticks in the ground that were now smoking.

Lihua slowly approached them, Panpan following close behind.

One woman looked to be about middle age, and the other looked to be old enough to be her mother. The middle-aged woman clutched a flier in her hand as she scanned the wall as though looking for an empty spot to place her flier.

"Did you lose your baby?" Lihua asked the woman.

Both of the women looked at Lihua and then gasped when they saw Panpan.

"Don't worry," Lihua said. "She's my friend. She won't hurt you."

The younger woman chuckled. "We heard about a girl

traveling with a panda. Maybe you will bring me good luck."

"I hope you find your baby," Lihua said.

"Oh," the woman said, looking at her flier. "She's not a baby anymore. She was lost many years ago. I put up a new flier every year in the hope that..." Her voice trailed off as her eyes watered.

"May I...?" Lihua asked as she reached for the flier. The woman handed it over.

When Lihua saw the birth date of the woman's missing daughter, her hands started to shake. It was the same birth date as the one carved into her bracelet. It couldn't be. She must have been dreaming again, but then she saw the name of the missing girl. Zhu'er. Pearl. Her adopted parents had called her Lihua—little flower—but her grandmother had always called her Little Pearl. Somehow, she had known. She had always known.

Lihua forced herself to look up from the flier and at the woman. As she stared at the woman's face, she saw her own looking back at her. It was older, yes. Sadder. Years of worry had etched deep lines along her brow and the edges of her lips, but she could not ignore that this face was one she already knew.

It was the face of her mother.

Lihua reached into her pocket and pulled out her bracelet. As she held it up, the woman gasped. She recognized it instantly.

"Pearl!" the woman cried.

"Mama!" Lihua exclaimed. She fell into her mother's arms and together they wept tears of joy.

CHAPTER TWENTY-ONE

"I cannot believe the little girl on the train with a panda was our little Zhu'er," the older woman said.

"Oh!" Lihua's mother said, finally pulling back from her daughter but not letting her go. "This is your grandmother."

For some reason, Lihua balked at that a little. She already had a grandmother. She didn't know if Nainai was alive or dead, and she was certain she would never see her again, but she would always consider Nainai to be a grandmother to her. However, as she looked into the old woman's face, and saw the tears of love and joy there, she knew this woman wanted nothing more than to be her grandmother as well. She forced a smile to her face and gave the old woman a hug.

"We never gave up," Lihua's grandmother said. "We always prayed you would return to us."

Lihua felt a pang of guilt at those words. If her adoptive parents had never told her about her past, she never would have known she had another family and could have continued to live a perfectly happy life. And yet, this family, one she had never known, would have lived in anguish on her behalf. But she couldn't change the past. Her adoptive family did tell her the truth and turned her away for it. Wasn't finding her birth family what she wanted? What she had traveled so far to find? Why was she still feeling so lost? So confused? So hurt and angry?

Panpan nuzzled Lihua's hand. Lihua kneeled down and wrapped her arms around the panda's neck. With her face deep in Panpan's fur, Lihua felt safe and comforted. Her heartbeat slowed and her emotions cooled.

"My panda," Lihua said. "I don't suppose you have a place she can stay? I can't bear to be parted from her."

"We have a small farm just outside of the city," her mother said. "We have a barn for the chickens that should be big enough for your dear panda."

"That sounds perfect," Lihua said, standing and giving a grateful smile.

Her mother wrapped her arms around her again and led her away from the wall.

"We have so much to catch up on," her mother said. "Where have you been all this time?"

"I was in a small village, way out west," Lihua said.

"Did you have a family there?" Her mother asked.

"Yes..." Lihua almost continued, telling her mother about how her adoptive parents threw her out when their son was born, but as she looked at her mother, whose face was beaming, she realized that the truth would bring her no comfort.

She thought about the little children she rescued in the woods and how she hoped they were well taken care of. Her mother, of course, would want to believe that all this time, her lost daughter was at least with a loving family who had taken good care of her. It would only cause her more pain to know that Lihua had lived a hard life mostly void of affection only to be tossed out onto the streets to fend for herself where she would have died had she not been taken in by a kindly panda. The last thing she wanted to do was cause her mother more pain, especially in this moment.

"Yes," Lihua repeated. "I had a family. My parents owned a noodle restaurant and I had a loving grandmother and a darling baby brother."

"That is wonderful," her mother said, squeezing her arms. "I have two brothers. They and their wives and children live on farms nearby. They will be so happy to meet you!"

"And what about my father?" Lihua asked, though she regretted it as soon as she saw tears well up and fall down her mother's cheeks. "I...I'm sorry. I should not have—"

"Don't apologize," her mother cut her off. "You didn't know. And I would have to tell you eventually. Your father died several years ago."

Lihua felt her own heart seize in her chest and she gasped. In all of her visions of how her reunion with her parents might go, she hadn't really considered that they might be dead. She thought she had either been kidnapped and her parents would be glad to have her back, or they had sold her and would not care that she had returned. She never imagined that her parents could have died. She was filled with a sudden pang of grief for the father she never knew.

"He never stopped loving you," her mother said. "And he never stopped looking for you. Every week, he would travel to the farthest reaches of the city in the hopes of finding you. He would go to the train station and ask people who were traveling if they had seen you."

"He sounds like a wonderful father," Lihua said.

"He was..." her mother said but seemed to be holding something back. Lihua looked at her mother curiously, but didn't push her to continue. She didn't want to say something that would upset her mother any further than she already had. But her mother saw the look on Lihua's face and forced herself to keep speaking.

"Your father blamed himself for losing you," her mother said. "He had taken you with him to the market. He was haggling with a seller. He said he had only turned his back to you for a moment, but then you were gone."

"It wasn't his fault," Lihua said. "A kidnapper, a trafficker, he took me and sold me to my parents. He was probably looking for an opportunity to steal children. It could have happened to anyone."

Lihua's mother nodded her head and wiped at her tears. "We know," she said. "Over the years, many people tried to comfort us with such knowledge. But how can one be comforted after the loss of a child?" She sighed and shook her head. "His heart broke that day, and it never mended. Eventually, it just stopped working altogether."

Lihua just stared straight ahead, but she tangled her fingers in Panpan's fur. Her father had died for the love of her. She never wanted to bring anyone sadness, especially her own parents. And now she would never meet this man who had loved her so completely. The loss of her father, and the knowledge that she was the cause of his death, was a pain she wasn't sure she could bear. She began to wish she had never been born. Then none of them would have suffered so much.

"But we are together now," Lihua's mother continued. "He would be so happy to know that you were safe and have now returned to us. Tonight, we can light incense and say prayers in his honor."

Lihua smiled and nodded. She had no desire to correct her mother's view of the past. There was nothing she could do to bring her father back. But maybe she could help his spirit find peace.

"I would like that," Lihua said.

"You must be starving," her mother said as they approached a brown brick farmhouse. It was bigger than she expected. Larger than the noodle shop she had grown up in. In front of the house was a large rice paddy, and all around them were rolling hills and green fields. They walked up several steps to the double doors. When her mother opened them, Lihua was surprised to see a large sitting room with comfortable chairs and an alter with a statue of Guanyin in the middle of it. There were doors on either side of the room leading to more rooms and a ladder that led to two rooms up above.

"This is a mansion!" Lihua mumbled, and her mother and grandmother laughed.

"We live very humbly," her mother said. "My brothers help us considerably. But if you think this dirt building is impressive, wait until you see the homes they live in."

Panpan was standing in the doorway sniffing the air.

"Where can Panpan sleep?"

"With the chickens," her mother said, slipping past Panpan and across the yard to a small brown brick and wooden shack. "I can have a farm boy bring up some fresh hay."

Panpan grunted as she saw the chicken coop, and Lihua didn't blame her. It looked like a dark, smelly little building, and Panpan was used to sleeping in the fresh night air. But she didn't want to offend her mother, who was kind enough to accept Panpan without question.

"Thank you," Lihua said. "It's perfect."

"I'll show you to your room as well," her mother said as she led her inside. "It's not much since we weren't expecting you, but..."

Lihua looked back at Panpan and shrugged as her mother led her back inside.

Late that night, Lihua looked out the window of her loft room at the stars up above. She couldn't sleep. Her stomach rumbled. She hadn't eaten much at dinner. The food was so spicy it set her mouth and stomach on fire! It wasn't the tingling, flavorful type of spicy she was used to, but a spicy that was too hot to eat. She did her best to eat what she could, but after a few bites, she had to lie and tell her mother that she wasn't hungry. She told her mother how she had been raised in a noodle shop and would cook food for them tomorrow with the last of her huajiao.

After dinner, they stayed up late talking about what life was like here in Changsha. There had been many changes over the years, but the communists were currently in charge. Her mother wasn't sure she trusted the communists, but the stability they had created in the area was a welcome change, she said. Lihua didn't understand all of what her mother told her, but she hoped she would soon make sense of it.

Eventually, her mother and grandmother retired to their own rooms, so Lihua went to her room. She had imagined that once she found her birth mother, she would never want to let her out of her sight again. But at the end of the night, she was glad for a moment alone. Her thoughts and emotions ran around wildly. One minute, she would be so grateful to be home, but in the next, she felt like a complete stranger, a fraud. This wasn't her home. Who were these people? With their strange accents and their inedible food. Where was she? Why was she even here?

Why wasn't she happy?

Lihua looked down and saw Panpan sitting outside the chicken coop. She waved down at her, and Panpan lifted her nose to the wind and sniffed. Lihua realized that she couldn't remember when she last slept in a bed in a house. She had become used to sleeping curled up with Panpan. So, she slipped out of her room, down the ladder, and out to the chicken coop.

"You can't sleep either?" she asked Panpan. Panpan grunted and snuffled Lihua's hand.

"Come on," Lihua said as she crouched down and walked into the chicken coop. "We can sleep in here together."

Panpan seemed to begrudgingly follow Lihua into the coop.

"I suppose we better get used to this place," Lihua said as she curled up in Panpan's fur. "This is our home now."

"Zhu'er!"

Lihua's eyes shot open. It took her a moment to realize her mother was calling her. She sat up quickly and looked around. Panpan was gone!

Lihua scrambled out of the chicken coop, banging her head on the low opening. She cursed as she rubbed her forehead and opened her eyes to the rising sun.

"What?" Lihua asked. "What's going on? Where's Panpan?"

"Oh! Zhu'er!" her mother cried, running to her and holding her tightly. "When I didn't see you in your room this morning, I thought you had disappeared again! Or worse, that you had never come home at all! That I had dreamed the whole thing!" Her mother held her so tightly, she almost couldn't breathe, but she didn't push her away. She could feel that her mother needed to hold her. And even though she had felt a bit overwhelmed the night before, she enjoyed being held as well. She supposed she was getting used to it.

"Where is Panpan?" Lihua asked again when her mother finally loosened her grip.

"I don't know," her mother said. "I haven't seen her."

Lihua felt a bit of panic in her stomach as she pulled away from her mother and looked around the yard, the rice paddies, and the hills surrounding the farm.

"Panpan!" she yelled. Then, off in the distance, in the trees, her eyes caught a glimpse of white in the shadows. Lihua took off toward her.

"Zhu'er!" her mother called, her voice tight and anxious.

"I'll be right back," Lihua said. "I promise."

Lihua ran into the woods, jumping over fallen branches and dodging leaves.

"Panpan!" she said when she caught up with her. "What are you doing out here?"

Panpan grunted and moved to continue walking through the woods, but Lihua stopped her.

"Where are you going?" Lihua asked. "We don't have to keep traveling. We are staying here now."

Panpan grumbled and nudged Lihua back toward the house.

"Come back with me," Lihua begged. "We can build you

a better house. One you won't have to share with the chickens."

Panpan sneezed and shook her head before turning to walk away again, but Lihua followed after her, falling to her knees in front of her.

"Are you really leaving?" Lihua asked, tears falling from her eyes. "After everything? You're all I have left!"

Panpan grunted and looked back toward the house. Then she leaned in and licked Lihua's face.

Lihua hugged Panpan tightly. "I would have died without you," she said. Panpan snuffled her hair and Lihua sat back. "But now that I have found my family, I suppose it is time for you to find yours. A panda can't live in a village, I guess."

Panpan groaned and nuzzled her head against Lihua's.

"I love you, Panpan," Lihua said. "I'll never forget you."

Panpan gave Lihua's face one last lick, then she ran off into the woods. Lihua stood and watched her go, feeling a little piece of her heart go with her.

Lihua waited for a long time, just in case Panpan changed her mind, but she knew she wouldn't. Panpan had done what she set out to do—make sure that Lihua was safe with her own family.

Finally, Lihua forced herself to turn back to the farmhouse.

When she emerged from the woods, her mother was still there watching for her with her brows knitted and her shawl pulled tightly around her. Lihua could see her visibly exhale when their eyes met. She thought her mother must not have taken a single breath since she pulled away from her and went into the woods. Even though they had only met hours before, Lihua could feel her mother's love pulling her forward. She ran to her mother and fell into her arms.

"She's gone," Lihua cried.

"I'm so sorry," her mother said as she held her tightly and ran her hands down her hair.

"Don't be," Lihua said. "I'm home, Mama."

The End

THANK YOU

Thank you for reading A Girl and Her Panda! If you enjoyed it, I hope you will leave a review. If you want to know when the next Animal Companions adventure is released, be sure to join my mailing list!
http://zoeygong.com/subscribe/

A GIRL AND HER ELEPHANT

books2read.com/elephantgirl

One girl risks everything to save the life of her friend...

All of the elephants wept as one of their own lay dying in childbirth. But Kanita, the daughter of the royal elephant trainer, refused to give up. With her own hands, she helped bring the baby elephant, Safi, into the world, beginning a lifelong friendship between a girl and her elephant.

But many of the villagers worried about the curse of the white elephant with the red birthmark across her face.

Raised in the mountains of northern Siam, Kanita's idyllic life is shattered when she is ordered to marry a much older man and leave her beloved yet cursed elephant behind. But Kanita's stubborn nature refuses to bow to her parents' wishes.

Kanita and Safi flee their village with the goal of redeeming Safi from her cursed reputation and cementing their bond, vowing to never be separated.

But the jungle is more dangerous than Kanita or Safi could have imagined.

Follow Kanita and Safi through the jungles of ancient Siam in a story of friendship, hope, and redemption.

A GIRL AND HER TIGER

books2read.com/tigergirl

She didn't plan on becoming a rebel...

After watching her parents serve in British households for her whole life, Priya had grown to despise every aspect of British colonialism. After an introduction to a British family in an attempt to secure a servant position of her own ends in disaster, Priya runs away to try and find a better life.

But she doesn't get far.

Alone on the streets of Bombay, Priya is kidnapped and taken captive aboard a smuggler's ship bound for the slave markets of the Americas.

And in the cage next to her – is a ferocious mama tiger named Nabhitha!

When Priya and the tiger see a chance for escape, will Priya dare to take it? Or will she end up the tiger's dinner?

Follow Priya and Nabhitha on a journey of courage and second chances.

ABOUT THE AUTHOR

ZOEY GONG was born and raised in rural Hunan Province, China. She has been studying English and working as a translator since she was sixteen years old. Now in her early twenties, Zoey loves traveling and eating noodles for every meal. She lives in Shenzhen with her cat, Jello, and dreams of one day disappointing her parents by being a Leftover Woman (剩女). Learn more at ZoeyGong.com.

facebook.com/ZoeyGongAuthor
goodreads.com/zoeygong
bookbub.com/authors/zoey-gong

ABOUT THE PUBLISHER

VISIT OUR WEBSITE
TO SEE ALL OF OUR HIGH QUALITY BOOKS:

http://www.redempresspublishing.com

Quality trade paperbacks, downloads, audio books, and books in foreign languages in genres such as historical, romance, mystery, and fantasy.

Made in the USA
Monee, IL
11 March 2024